Leaving
Barringer
A Blackstone Family Novel

TINA MARTIN

The Dilemma...

Before we married, my husband and I dated for two years. We learned each other. We knew we wanted to be together forever and have a family. We wanted two children. Five years later, we don't have any children. He says he's not ready. That he's busy building his brand to be distracted by a child right now. I'm thirty-four years old. I'm not getting any younger and neither are my eggs. I shouldn't have to beg my husband for a child. My question is, do I stay and continue with my efforts in convincing him that I want a child? Should I leave and seek my own happiness? Or should I give him an ultimatum – give me a baby or I'm out?

-Calista Blackstone

The Blackstone Family

PARENTS: Theodore (Theo) Blackstone & Elowyn Blackstone

CHILDREN:

Bryson Blackstone [Age 38]
  -Married to Kalina Blackstone
  -Owns Blackstone Tree Service

Barringer (Barry) Blackstone [Age 36]
  -Married to Calista Blackstone
  -CEO of Blackstone Financial Services Group (BFSG)

Garrison (Gary) Blackstone [Age 34]
  -Married to Vivienne Blackstone
  -Director of Finance at Blackstone Financial Services Group (BFSG)

Everson Blackstone [Age 32]
  -Married to June Blackstone
  -Business Management Analyst (Freelance)

Candice (Candy) Blackstone [Age 28]
  -Single and looking
  -Manager of Customer Relations at Blackstone Financial Services Group (BFSG)

COUSINS:

Rexford Blackstone [Age 37]
 -Single and *always* looking
 -Police Officer

Colton Blackstone [Age 33]
 -Single
 -Painter, owns Blackstone Painting, LLC

~*~
*If you never had to fight for it, how do
you know you really want it?*
~*~

Leaving Barringer
(A Blackstone Family Novel)

Chapter 1

Calista Blackstone scanned the interior of her bedroom one last time before zipping up the large, black suitcase that rested on top of their king bed – a suitcase she had packed full of her clothes. Not *all* of her clothes. Just enough. The essentials. Two weeks' worth for now. She would have to get the rest later.

Blinking back tears while feeling pressure build in her throat, she forced away memories of all the times she and Barringer had made love in this bed, although she couldn't recall a recent instance. Then again, there was that one time a few months ago, but there was nothing memorable about that occasion. Nothing to brag about to her girlfriends if she was into that sort of thing. (She wasn't). The intimacy, if you can call it *intimacy*, was cold, to-the-minute quick, sorely lacking and wham-bam*ish*, followed by Barringer snoring loudly shortly thereafter. There was no cuddling. No, I love you. No good night kiss. No nothing. And she lay awake, yet again, staring at ceiling, wondering how they got to this point while listening to him snore like a bear in hibernation.

That memory alone was enough to push her to the door, but she drifted in thought again, forcing herself to remember some of the good times. Like when they would stay in bed all day, order takeout and go right back to bed. Or when they'd share popcorn and watch movies together in *that* bed. Or when she would lie against his chest while they watched football or the ten o'clock news. And what about the cool evenings when he would hold her. When he'd run his fingers through her hair while they talked about their days. When lovemaking was more than, let's-hurry-up-and-get-this-over-with-so-I-can-go-to-sleep, but actually meant something. The memories remained, but those days of marital bliss were long gone. The shipped had sailed. The train had officially left the station.

Still, it was a struggle to go. It was easy to threaten to leave your spouse, but when it came down to it, when actions were supposed to speak louder than words, sometimes the action didn't speak up loud enough. Calista wanted to change that. And she did.

This was the fifth time she packed a suitcase this year. Fifth. Would the fifth time be the charm? Not necessarily. There was nothing pleasant about leaving her husband. It's not like she wanted to leave Barringer, but he wasn't giving her much of a choice these days.

She could admit that the first time she had threatened to leave, it was just that – a threat. She hoped it would be a wake-up call for him that she wasn't happy. It worked, for a few weeks. Barringer would come home at a decent hour, try to watch a movie with her or do something she enjoyed like going for a walk, but she could tell he had everything else on his mind besides being with her. His body was there. His mind was some place else.

The second, third and fourth attempts at leaving were legit, and they all came within weeks of each other. Calista was pumped up and ready each time. She'd tried to build up enough courage to leave, but failed, going through the emotions of leaving. It was one thing to huff and puff and say what you were going to do. It was another actually following through with it. Could she follow through with it this time? Could she live her own life apart from Barringer? Was she not doing that already?

Back to the present attempt to leave – attempt number five...

This time would be different. Unlike those other failed attempts, she made preparations for this one. While Barringer was busy devoting his time, his life, to making deals and nursing important business relationships at Blackstone Financial Services Group, working well into the night every day of the week, she was at home planning. Strategizing. She'd gone on two job interviews (both jobs looked promising) and she went apartment shopping, finding a one-bedroom place near Kalina and Bryson's home. She already paid the rent for the first month as well as the security deposit. The place was hers.

Last week, she bought a new cell phone and attached service to it, no longer desiring to be connected to their family plan. *Family plan...what a joke.* She even visited some car lots. She didn't know how Barringer would react when he found out she was really leaving this time, so she took preemptive measures to check out a few vehicles in case he flipped out and decided to take the Lexus away from her. He very well could have. After all, the car was in his name. Registered to him. He paid for it, like he paid for everything else. It's the way he wanted it.

Barringer was one of those ol' school men, not in a gentlemanlike way, but in a rigid orderly way. His belief was that a man was supposed to be the breadwinner of the family. The provider. Didn't matter that Calista had a bachelor's degree in healthcare administration and was an intelligent woman with a bright future in her career field. Before they married, he and Calista had come to an agreement – that instead of her pursuing a career, she would be a homemaker, the mother to their children. The dutiful wife who managed the household, cooked, cleaned, made sure bills were paid on time and any other 'menial tasks' (his words) he deemed out of scope for a husband. Calista agreed to forego her career to do just that. Why wouldn't she? She was happy. In love. Married to the man of her dreams. She'd snagged *the* Barringer Blackstone.

A manly man, he was a little rough around the edges, but still together enough to work in corporate. He was solidly built – iron muscles, tight abs, a killer smile and tall stature. He kept his black hair cut to a shadow as well as the mustache above a set of eye-catching, irresistible lips. And the man could rock a suit like nobody's business. He dressed nice during work and play, although nowadays, she rarely saw him in *play* clothes. He was strictly business. Owned more suits than she had dresses. Twenty-four hours a day, seven days a week, Barringer was a business man. A provider, like he said he'd be. But nearly six years later, Calista wasn't the woman she wanted to be.

She wanted to be a mother, but they didn't have any children. She wanted to be a wife, but to who? Their grand, four-thousand-square-feet home? She certainly wasn't a wife to Barringer, her absentee husband. How could she be a wife to a man who was never there? It was like baking an apple pie with no apples. Sure, you could still bake it, but could you really call it an apple pie if you put no apples in it?

She sighed. What did she have to show for herself after six years of marriage? Not a thing. She had herself, hurt feelings and regret of putting faith in a man who didn't hold up his end of the bargain. Well, enough was enough.

She looked around again, thinking about how her new apartment was about the same size as their master bedroom. Leaving Barringer was a downgrade in her lifestyle, but that was okay. She'd survive. Funny how material things meant absolutely nothing when you had no one to share them with. When you were lonely. Depressed. Sick and tired of being taken for granted. The apartment was looking better and better.

She sat on the bed when her stomach began aching – her nerves getting the best of her. She hid her face behind her hands and blew a breath. If she could only force herself to stop thinking about it so much, she'd be gone already. Instead, she began wondering what people would think. If she actually went through with attempt number five and left Barringer, what would her parents think? His parents? Neighbors? Friends they had in common. What would happen to her relationships with her sisters-in-law, who were also her best girlfriends – Vivienne, Kalina, June and Candice? What would they say if she actually left Barringer this time?

Calista pushed out a breath. Attempt five was hard, but it had to be done. Why should she be concerned about what people thought, anyway? They didn't have to live her miserable life. They didn't know the pain and loneliness she felt every day. The resentment that churned deep within her soul from the lies she'd been hanging on to from the man who was supposed to love her. Leaving Barringer, her husband of six years was the hardest thing she ever had to do, but she couldn't continue on like this – miserable and unhappy – while watching everyone around her live blissfully and in love. Her brother-in-law, Bryson, had recently married Kalina, so they were all over each other, lovey-dovey, still in the honeymoon phase. She was happy for them, but jealous at the same time. She wanted that serendipitous feeling of being in love again. Vivienne and Garrison were days away from welcoming their first child. She wanted a child, too.

She thought about how they'd often feign happiness in public but the fake smiles and phony public displays of affection wasn't enough glue to hold their situation together behind closed doors, at least as far as Calista was concerned. Barringer seemed to go with the flow, expend all of his time and energy in his work and pretend nothing was wrong.

She used to be the queen of pretending, but even that had worn off. She pinched tears from the corner of her eyes. Her vows meant something to her, but obviously they didn't mean a thing to Barringer. His loyalty was aligned with protecting the interest and affairs of his father's precious company – the company where he spent most of his days, Blackstone Financial Services Group. Everything else had to take a backseat. Even her.

Calista sniffled. She'd rode in the backseat for four of the six years they'd been married. It was time for a change – time to upgrade to the driver's seat – beginning now.

Chapter 2

Crushed and at the lowest of the low, Barringer stepped inside his home, tossing the black jacket of his Givenchy suit to the white bench in the foyer. His day was one he didn't want to repeat, having lost his company's largest client. The Blakeney Agency – a company which boasted offices in every major U.S. city and employed well over five-hundred thousand employees in their corporate offices and various subsidiaries – had decided to take their business elsewhere.

Barringer pleaded with them, offered up every perk he could think of, but the CEO already had his sights set on a new finance firm, one with innovative business solutions which Blackstone Financial Services Group had yet to offer. The result: the worst day of Barringer's career since his father had entrusted him with the operation of the company. He'd failed today. Failed miserably.

He'd given The Blakeney Agency his best effort but his best wasn't good enough to convince them to stay.

Disgusted with himself for being a failure, he left the office soon after his meeting with Blakeney had concluded. He didn't take the time to meet with his sister Candice the customer relations manager at BFSG or his brother Garrison, director of finance. He just left. Got his briefcase, slid on a pair of RayBans, hopped in the driver seat of his Porsche and dipped.

His breath caught every time he tried to breathe normally. Legs were too nervous for him to sit down. His head pounded too fiercely to think right now, so there was no use in attempting to come up with a plan to dig his way out of this and strategize the company's future. Not right now. He wasn't in the right frame of mind. Right now, he needed a drink. He found that drink in the well-stocked wet bar in his man cave. Tequila. He poured a shot and tossed it back to his throat. No lime. Just straight. He followed with another one, lowering the shot glass on the granite countertop. That's when he heard commotion upstairs.

Calista.

Completely occupied by his midday crisis, he'd forgotten she was here. He rubbed his chin, trying to remember if he saw her Lexus parked out front. Or maybe she'd parked in the garage.

He scrubbed his hand down his pre-five

o'clock shadow, thinking about her. In addition to his now crumbling company, his marriage, like Southern Comfort served chilled, was on the rocks. Calista had been giving him the silent treatment for days on end, threatening to leave him yet again, a threat he easily dismissed. Problems at work took precedence over problems at home. Without work, he (they) wouldn't have a home. Besides, Calista had cried wolf so many times, she made the little boy from the fairytale look like an angel. Her threats to leave him over their marital issues were nothing but mere cries for attention. That's why he didn't bother putting much stock into the latest threat from a week ago. She wasn't going anywhere. He gave her everything she wanted. Why would she walk away from it all?

When he heard her coming down the stairs, he stepped out of the man cave to see why she was making so much noise. Their stairs weren't creaky. What was the loud thump he heard every second or so? He got his answer when she finally came into view for it was then he saw the large suitcase behind her.

His heart dropped to his feet. His chest was already tight from work-related anxiety. Now, it grew even tighter. His wife was heading for the front door with a suitcase big enough to hide a body. A frown dented his forehead. *Here we go again.* He stepped in full view asking, "What are you doing?"

Ignoring him, Calista continued to the door. What was he doing here anyway? He was supposed to be at work. This wasn't part of the plan.

"Calista," he said, raising his voice.

Oh, now you see me when, for three days, you haven't said a word to me. Pulling the suitcase determined to reach the front door without a confrontation ensuing, she kept her head straight. Eyes aimed for the foyer. Mind sharp, seconds away from reaching her goal.

"Calista, you need to stop playing games," Barringer said as he stepped into the living room, charging behind her.

"I'm not playing games with you, Barringer," she said evenly but with a resolve that had him nervous.

Okay, so she was serious *this* time. He could feel it in his gut. She wasn't crying wolf. She was running for the hills, escaping a marriage which he knew had problems but chose to ignore. Ignore a problem long enough and this is what you end up with – an even bigger problem. An unhappy wife. An unhappy life. He had to stop her.

Calista continued on to the door, proud of herself for finally taking a stand and doing so without becoming overly emotional. She couldn't cry. She was too focused to cry. Too fed up to shed a tear. That's why she couldn't look at him. She would surely lose it if their gazes connected. Furious at the man for neglecting her, she still loved him. Would always love him. But some things couldn't be tolerated.

Hoping to reach the door and get outside

before he had a chance to stop her, she recklessly pulled the suitcase behind her. The wheel of the suitcase snagged a rug in the foyer that, in turn, caused a lamp to fall from a black, half-moon table, shattering onto the floor.

"Calista!" Barringer yelled, broken bits of porcelain crackling underneath his leather shoes. He gestured towards the mess with an opened hand. "Look what you've done!"

Calista lifted a brow. Was he for real? "Yeah, look what I've done, because a broken lamp is more important to you than your wife leaving you, right, Barry?" she said with a bitter edge to her voice.

His nostrils flared. "You know what Calista...my patience is really starting to wear thin with your antics."

"Antics?" Somehow a smile came to her face like the sun bursting through thick, gray clouds for a brief moment. This was it. A moment of clarity. The confirmation she needed that she was heading in the right direction. For the door. "Whatever, Barry. I'm out."

He frowned. "You're out? What do you mean, you're out?"

"You're a smart man, Barry. Figure it out. I'm standing at the front door with a suitcase."

He began taking slow, intimidating steps towards her, crushing bits of shattered porcelain underneath his size fourteen Canali's. "I have had the worst day of my professional life, and I have to come home to deal with this?"

This? Calista's frown deepened. "Oh, I'm

sorry I'm not leaving you at your convenience, you selfish bastard!" She blew a breath and looked up at man who towered over her. "You know what, Barringer...I couldn't care less about your bad day when I have endured years of bad days with you. So why don't you save your pity party for someone else because I have had it! I'm done. You don't have to *deal* with me anymore." Anger blazed from her eyes, but were softened by tears she failed to hold in. She swiped them away, grabbed a hold of her suitcase and reached for the doorknob. She was mere steps away from freedom – a new beginning. A husbandless start. Feeling powerful and in control of her destiny. So why did her legs nearly buckle when she felt Barringer grip her arm while pulling the suitcase from her grasp?

"Calista, just stop," he said in a more reasonable tone. "We can work this out. Don't do this to us."

"It's too late for that," Calista said, moving, pulling, yanking her arm to free herself from his grasp. "Let me go, Barry."

"No," he said, pulling her closer, his hands settling at her waist. "Look at me."

She refused. She couldn't. Staring into his dark, pleading eyes always did a number on her. She had to resist falling under his spell. She couldn't look at him if she expected to walk through those double doors.

"Cali, look at me," he said in a seductive whisper. "Please."

Calista closed her eyes. She missed his

captivating whispers. Missed the smell of his breath. His skin. The way his hands felt gripped around her waist. *Stay focused, Calista. Don't fall for his empty promises. The marriage won't get any better. It'll only get worse.*

"I know things haven't been right for some time but it'll all work out, baby." His hands left her waist to settle at the sides of her face. He stared longingly at her while her eyes were closed. "Cali, open your eyes."

She opened them, slowly, connecting her gaze with his. When she saw the fear in his eyes, she knew she was a goner.

"We can't give up, baby," he told her. "We can't."

Calista swallowed hard. He was doing it again. Every time she tried to leave him in the past, he'd hit her with his we-can-work-this-out speech. As it stood, they hadn't made love in months. He was always busy working, or he was too tired and if one of those excuses wouldn't do, he'd find something else to avoid the bedroom. And every time they did make love, he'd be sure to take precautions to ensure she wouldn't become pregnant.

"Calista," he said, nudging her chin up with a gentle touch of his index finger. "It'll get better. I promise. We're just going through a rough patch."

"A rough patch doesn't last for four years," she said with a weak, broken voice. The strength she had, the resolve that was once there, was gone.

"We'll get through it. Trust me."

"Barry—"

"Trust me." He lowered his lips to hers, feeling resistance at first. Shortly thereafter, she caved, fell into his embrace and kissed him back with as much desperation as he kissed her.

Before she could attempt to offer up a second round of resistance, she felt herself being lifted from the floor while Barringer carried her upstairs to the bedroom – the same room she'd silently said her goodbyes to a few minutes ago. The room she was sure she'd never see again. That was short lived.

Actually, she wasn't paying much attention to the room. After clothes and shoes went flying – his shirt tossed this way, her clothes scattered that way – Calista was lying on her back, looking at Barringer hovering over her. It had been months. At every point where his body touched hers, she quivered. She felt like she'd pass out when his warm lips brushed against her neck – the feeling so intense, she could barely breathe. Why did he have to make her feel this way when she was at her breaking point? Why?

"Are you okay?" he asked softly against her ear.

"Yes," she said, spellbound.

He ran his fingers through her long hair, staring into her wide, bright eyes. Sad eyes. He hoped to make them happy again. "Sure?"

"Yes."

He stopped kissing her neck to look at her.

To connect their eyes. "Are you sure you're okay?"

"Yes, Barringer," she whimpered, feeling his body connect and collide with hers between the halfway point of love and insanity – a joining so grand, so needed, it had her reciting vows in her head.

What God has yoked together, let no man put a part.

He stared at her face as he slowly settled, nibbling at his bottom lip at the immense pleasure tearing through him. All the times she wanted to leave him had ended this way – with him owning her, loving her like he'd never see her again, like it was their first time touching each other. Like he loved her and only realized it when he came close to losing her.

Capturing her mouth with his, he took more soft kisses before greed turned them into ravenous ones. He missed her, and he realized he'd let work come between them. But there was something else eating away at his conscience – a secret he'd kept from her before they were even married. One he refused to think about right now. At this precise moment, he had to save his marriage and to his way of thinking, if he loved her hard enough, moved deep enough, kissed her with undeniable passion and took his time making love to her, he would buy himself more time to straighten things out. That's all she needed, right? To know he loved her? To feel that love? He hoped so.

Releasing her mouth, he left tender kisses

against her face, down to her earlobe and neck, feeling her body quiver beneath him. He liked that because he knew she liked it. Her body was telling him so. The airy gasps and soft moans escaping between her lips told him so. He was on the right path, seducing her to stay, desperately wanting nothing more than to save his marriage. If she could just feel how much he loved her, how freely he was giving himself to her, how methodical and attentive he was to her needs, maybe she'd stay. He should've been attentive to her needs before, but better late than never.

He frowned. He didn't want to think about this while he was making love to his wife. That's how he found himself in this predicament to start with.

"I love you, Cali," he whispered, gazing down at her, slowly moving on top of her. "I love you." That was true. Barringer loved his wife. He was loyal to Calista. He didn't have roving eyes. Late nights at the office weren't because there was another woman in the picture. He loved Calista and only her. But he also loved success and wealth. His problem was, he didn't know how to prioritize, perhaps the reason he also lost the Blakeney account. Candice warned him a few months ago that Blakeney was hinting at looking for a new firm once their contract ended. Vying for new business, he ignored her, put it on the backburner and now, he'd lost them. He put Calista and her desire to have a family on the backburner, too. But, like Blakeney, he couldn't lose her.

Calista closed her eyes when she felt tears well up in them. Barringer said he loved her. She knew that already. Whether or not he loved her wasn't the issue which made their problem a unique one. It was Calista's belief he didn't know how to love her. He knew how to provide for her, and he was demonstrating how well and thorough he could *make* love to her. But he really didn't know how to love her.

A tear escaped her eye, rolled slowly towards her ear as she'd reached an epiphany. Her husband didn't know how to love her.

"I'm not hurting you, am I?"

How could she answer truthfully while they were making love? Physically he wasn't hurting her. Mentally, he was doing a number on her. No woman, no wife wanted to feel like she had to take extreme measures to get her husband's attention. Was he making love to her only so he could buy himself a couple more months, or was this genuine? The fact that she didn't know was a problem.

Moving slow yet still dominating, fueling her desire for more of him, Barringer remembered when lovemaking used to be frequent. When they'd gotten married, they couldn't keep their hands off of each other. What happened?

"Barry," Calista gasped, attempting to tighten the grip she had on his large biceps.

Something about hearing her whisper his name while feeling her squeeze him boosted his desire to please her to the fullest. She needed this. They both did.

Nibbling on her bottom lip, she kept her eye

closed when sensations washed through her, nearly drowning her with passion. She lost all sense. All control, quivering underneath him.

"Calista," he said gruffly, his body locking up and letting go as he gave her all he had. He threw his head back and toppled over, emptying his mind, soul and heart into her all at once. He wanted to give her his all, wanted to be the perfect husband for her, but he knew his all would never be enough because while he could give her just about anything in the world she wanted, he couldn't give her the one thing she wanted more than anything – a baby. According to his doctor, he was sterile, and he could never find the right words or the right time to tell Calista that.

Chapter 3

Calista watched Barringer as he slept. It was only a few minutes after ten, but he was out. Cold. She scanned his features. He looked thick and muscular, something he could hide well in his suits, but lying here naked, she had a full view of him. His thighs, butt and legs were all toned and sculpted to perfection. He was overpoweringly male and highly intelligent. That's what attracted her to him – he was strong and smart – so she knew he'd be a good protector and provider. And she loved the fact that he was driven. Had ambition and craved success.

How ironic.

The same thing which made her love him, was the very thing that caused discontentment in their marriage.

She sighed heavily and closed her eyes. She'd made love to him just hours ago. Even when she knew it wouldn't change her mind –

knew that even through her moment of weakness, nothing he could do at this point would sway her – she made love to him. She knew he would try to seduce her into staying, which was part of the reason why she planned her grand escape before he was due to be home. He'd worked until eleven at night almost every day this week, but *this* day, the day he supposedly had the worst day of his professional career, he'd come home early and caught her coming downstairs with a suitcase.

Weird how those two incidents coincided with each other. It almost didn't seem like a coincidence, like he was supposed to be home early *that* day. Like the universe was giving him a nudge in the right direction. He lost a client which resulted in him coming home early which, in turn, resulted in him stopping her attempt to leave.

His idea of stopping her was making love to her. Not sitting down, talking – arguing if they had to – over the problems at hand. He wanted to Band-Aid their issues with temporary pleasure.

And she fell for it.

So if she knew what his tactic would be why did she sleep with him? The answer was simple.

She loved her husband. He was her world. Her everything. Before life got complicated, when they were blissfully in love and he was an employee at BFSG instead of the person running it, they were actually happy. Granted he wasn't a millionaire then, but she didn't need him to be. The richest people in life were usually the brokest. People could live comfortably without being rich. They were financially stable before the millions, lived in a smaller home and had time for each other, something they sorely lacked now.

When life was simpler, he made it home in time for dinner, or he would pick her up and go somewhere for dinner. He did little things to help out around the house, like fold clothes, vacuum, even cook. It was just him and her. Barringer and Calista. *He* was her everything, her world, and that was a major part of her problem. Their problem. Her life revolved around him. Who was Calista Blackstone besides, Barringer Blackstone's wife?

She'd given up her dreams to be his wife. She was looking forward to following in her mother's footsteps and working behind the scenes in the healthcare field, assisting people. It would be a fulfilling career, one in which she could be proud of. But Barringer didn't want her to work. He wanted her to be a stay-at-home mom. Six years later, she was a stay-at-home wife. She hoped she would be a mother at some point because there wasn't a greater job in the world than being a mother. It was a privilege. Rewarding. Unfortunately, she wouldn't get to experience being a mother, because while she held up her end of the deal and took care of the household, Barringer hadn't given her a baby. Now she wasn't sure she wanted his baby, being on the verge of leaving and all.

Calista eased up from the bed, careful not to disturb the mattress too much. She didn't want to wake him. She looked at him when she was standing next to the bed. He slept soundly. She doubted a fire alarm could wake him. He was out, and she had to use that to her advantage. She picked up her clothes from the hardwood floor then stepped into the bathroom, feeling knots form in her stomach, nervous she might get caught again. As she pulled her panties up her legs, she thought about how, two weeks ago, she'd cooked a pot of roast beef, one of Barringer's favorite meals to perfection, made a thick, creamy bowl of garlic mashed potatoes and a fresh garden salad. In their expansive dining room – large because they regularly entertained family as well as Barringer's work executives – she lit candles, played soft jazz music and served him up his favorite meal. It was one of their good days. The kind of day that gave her a glimmer of optimism that maybe, just maybe, they would make it through marriage somehow. Every married couple had problems. No marriage was perfect. Life was okay. Things were off balance but they were manageable – at least *that* particular day they were.

They had talked about their respective days, something they hadn't done in some time. She told him how she'd set up the appointment with his cousin Colton to have the guest bedrooms downstairs painted. Passionate plum was the color she chose for one and the other would be refresh*mint* green.

When it was his turn to talk about his day, he chose to disclose how one of their biggest competitors was trying to steal their largest client. She thought it was odd for him to bring up something work-related since he usually never talked to her about business. Apparently, the candles and champagne had relaxed him enough to let his guard down. She figured she'd use that to her advantage and talk about children. She was the one to bring up that subject. Never him. Always her. Deciding to dive in, she asked him what she always asked – when they would try to get pregnant.

Suddenly his relaxed demeanor became one of irritation. He poured more champagne in his flute and said, "Come on, Cali. Don't ruin our night bringing up babies again. Let's enjoy each other right now."

And that was the end of that.

Just like tonight was the end of them.

FULLY DRESSED, CALISTA emerged from the bathroom, looking over at the bed to make sure Barringer was still sleeping. Due to the variations of shadows in the room, she couldn't get a full view of his face, but he wasn't moving and she could hear him snoring. He was still sleeping, thank God. Now she could make a clean getaway.

She quietly exited the bathroom, stepped out into the hallway and eased the door closed like a mother not wanting to wake a sleeping infant.

Afterwards, she carefully descended the stairs. Halfway down, she began seeing memories flash in her mind with each step:

> *Step* – the smile Barringer had on his face as he walked towards her on their wedding day
> *Step* – their one-year anniversary in Maui
> *Step* – an epic five-hour road trip from Wilmington to the Biltmore Inn at Asheville
> *Step* – camping in the backyard
> *Step* – running to the car in the rain after leaving one of their favorite restaurants
> *Step* – the family dinners
> *Step* – the lovemaking

Once at the bottom of the staircase, she looked up once more, her way of saying a final goodbye to her husband. To their house. To the memories. The pictures. The *what ifs*. Walking over the broken porcelain in the foyer, listening as it crackled underneath her shoes, she grabbed a hold of the suitcase handle, pulling it out of the door behind her.

Chapter 4

Releasing a deep breath that did nothing to calm the ache brewing at the front of her head, Calista stepped into her new home, a one-bedroom apartment across town, away from her old home – Barringer's home. She needed to be across town. When she had first started looking for a place to live, she knew she couldn't be near Barringer's house. It would be too much temptation to go running back to him, and at this point, that was not an option. She'd tried to work things out with him in the past, and they always ended up right back where they started after he supposedly tried to make things better.

She didn't tell the girls she was leaving Barringer. They knew about the strain in their marriage. Strangers could see the disconnect between them, so she knew the family was well aware, Kalina especially. She had confided in Kalina about some things, but she didn't want to be the woman who gave a play-by-play of everything that was going on in her relationship – good or bad. And she didn't want Barringer to know where she was living. At least for the first few weeks. She needed the time to decompress and detoxify from the strain of being his wife while transitioning into a better version of herself. She didn't know how she would keep her location a secret in Wilmington where everyone knew the Blackstone family, but she had no choice but to try.

She returned to her car, took a clothes basket out of the trunk which contained hair products, body washes, shampoos – a medley of personal care items. She had put the basket in the car before Barringer arrived. She had also packed a hamper full of towels and there had been a bag of shoes, another suitcase full of clothes and the bigger suitcase in the backseat – the one Barringer caught her dragging downstairs. She could still see the desperate look in his eyes when he realized she was attempting to leave again. Now that she had, she felt freedom, anticipating her new life and what it would feel like to be herself again and not just *his* wife. Starting over was exciting, but it came with its fair share of guilt. Now she had to wonder if she'd done enough to save the marriage – if leaving him was the right thing to do. Was she too hasty in her decision to go? She laid out the reasons:

1. Barringer was never there

2. She was lonely
3. She wanted children/he avoided the topic
4. Barringer wasn't himself anymore/he was always stressed about work
5. She didn't see how the situation could improve

Her leaving seemed to benefit him more than it did her. He was the one who didn't want children. He wanted to spend all of his time at work. He was never home. Now he was free to do whatever he wanted. And she would be free to start over and do what she wanted.

Calista lazily sat on the beige-carpeted floor in the living room. This would be more work than she realized, but what was the alternative? Be miserable with a man she'd become invisible to? Who took her for granted? It was better to be alone than with someone who didn't appreciate your worth. That's why she knew she had to make a clean break. Now wasn't the time for regrets. She had to stand on her own two feet and do this for herself. Leaving Barringer wasn't a cry for attention. It was the act of a woman who knew her worth – who knew she deserved better.

Chapter 5

In the morning, she woke up groggy, opened her eyes and quickly sprang upright, listening as her bones snapped, crackled and popped like Rice Crispies. Oh, that's right – she was in her new apartment. Exhausted, she'd forgotten. She rubbed her neck as she sat on the floor in the middle of the living room. Her eyes caught sight of the two folded towels she used for a pillow and the one she'd spread across her body like a blanket. No wonder she had a crook in her neck. She rubbed her neck a little more, attempting to work out the kinks.

When leaving one's husband, you must pack a pillow and blanket.

Continuing to massage the right side of her neck, she looked at her phone. First, she noticed the time was 11:08 a.m., then she saw the missed calls – twelve of them – all from Barringer. And he'd left voicemails and text messages, none of which she cared to listen to or read. She had to remain focused. Besides, there was a lot she had to get done today.

She needed to buy food, and she definitely needed a bed. She wouldn't be able to take another night of sleeping on the floor. A bed was a must. Living room furniture could wait for now.

Then there was Vivienne's party...

Kalina came up with the idea to throw Vivienne a party before she had the baby – not a baby shower party but a last hoorah before Vivienne transitioned into motherhood. Before the exhaustion that would come from 2:00 a.m. feedings, sore nipples from breastfeedings and midnight diaper changes. Diaper changes every hour and a half. For Vivienne, the gathering would be a final night with the ladies before little Garrison junior arrived.

Calista thought about not going to the party. Barringer was certain to have gone completely insane by then, wondering where she was and why she wasn't answering her phone. There was a good chance he'd crash Vivienne's party looking for her. Why ruin the girl's good time because she couldn't get her life straight? Then she remembered something – she was starting over and stepping out on her own. Such being the case, she couldn't let Barringer dictate her whereabouts. She was separated from him, not his family. Those women – Kalina, June, Vivienne and Candice were her best friends. Her only friends. She would support them no matter what, just like they supported her.

Chapter 6

Barringer held the phone to his ear, listening to ring after ring after heart-stopping ring. Calista wouldn't pick up. He dialed the number again, pacing the living room floor at Everson's house. Tonight was card game night for the fellas, but Barringer wasn't in the mood for card games or any other games. He had arrived two hours early, going off about how he couldn't get in touch with Calista. He knew she was gone when he got up this morning, jogged downstairs and saw the missing suitcase. He confirmed it when he checked the garage and didn't see her car. Where exactly had she run off to?

Barringer slid his phone in the front pocket of his slacks. "She won't even answer her phone, man," he told Everson. "I don't get it." Oh, he got it, all right. Calista had officially left him and he knew it. Could feel it in the pit of his stomach. Would his pride prevent him from telling his brother what was really going on?

"Barry, calm down, man," Everson said with a slight chuckle. "This is Calista we're talking about. I'm sure there's a logical explanation for this. Maybe her cell phone battery died or—"

"No." Barringer shook his head. "When I call, the phone rings which means it's on. It's not going straight to voicemail, Everson. It's ringing."

"Okay, then maybe it's on silent or vibrate," Everson said casually.

"I've been trying to call her since six o'clock this morning. It's now after four in the afternoon. Don't you think she would've looked at her phone by now, even if it was set to silent or vibrate? Wouldn't she have called me back?"

"You have a point," Everson said, crossing his arms. "Well, could there be someone else?"

Barringer glared at his brother. "No, there's no one else."

"Hey, I'm just throwing out all possible scenarios. Married people cheat. That's not a farfetched notion."

It took all Barringer had to restrain himself from snatching the beer bottle out of Everson's hand and clocking him over the head with it. "It *is* farfetched for my woman. I know Calista. She's not a cheater."

"Okay, my bad," Everson told him. "Why don't you have a seat? I'll get you a beer."

Barringer snatched out a chair, sat down and said, "Don't want a beer."

"Well, you're getting one whether you want it or not."

Barringer buried his face in his hands. He'd called Calista more times than he wanted to admit. Left her a dozen text messages. She wasn't trying to call him back. He knew she wouldn't call him. He shook his head. How could he think making love would pacify her into staying? Why didn't he give their marriage a little more effort?

"Here you go, bruh," Everson said, setting the beer on the table in front of Barringer.

"Thanks." Barringer popped the top off the bottle, took a long pull from it then looked over at Everson and said, "She left me, Everson."

Everson frowned. "Come again."

"Calista left me. She's gone, and I have no idea where she is." There, he said it. It felt good to get it off of his chest, but it didn't solve the mystery of her whereabouts.

Too antsy to remain sitting, Barringer stood up and began pacing the floor near the table.

"What do you mean she *left* you?" Everson asked. "Why would Calista leave you?"

As he was asking, the doorbell sounded.

Everson rolled his wrist to check his watch as he walked to the door. Who was it now? He got his answer when he opened the door to see Bryson standing there. *Is everybody coming early tonight or what?*

"You're here early, too," Everson said, as Bryson walked in.

"Yeah...figured since the women were doing their thing this evening, I'd come on over. Didn't I see Barry's car out front?"

"Yep. He's in the kitchen, and he's not in a

good mood," Everson said, evenly. "You've been warned."

"Thanks for the heads up. I wondered how he was taking the loss of The Blakeney Agency."

"Trust me...the loss of Blakeney is not what has him riled up at the moment."

"Then what does?" Bryson asked as they walked side-by-side to the kitchen.

"You'll find out soon enough."

When Bryson stepped into the kitchen and saw the distress on his brother's face, he knew, right away, Barringer's problem was woman-related. When a man and woman saw eye-to-eye, a relationship, a marriage, could be imperfectly perfect. When something was amiss, a man would have the look Barringer had on his face right now. His features were tight, eyes a hint of beige, glossed over by worry.

"What's up, Barry?" Bryson greeted him.

"Hey, Bryce," he said unenthused. He wasn't in the mood for small talk. Not when he had no idea where his wife was.

"What's going on?" Bryson asked.

Barringer dug his hands in his pockets and said, "Calista left me."

Bryson raised his brows though he wasn't the least bit surprised. He saw it coming from a mile away.

"You don't seem surprised," Everson told Bryson.

"That's because I'm not," Bryson said, walking to the fridge, grabbing a beer. He walked over to the table and sat down across from Everson.

Barringer sat down, too.

Bryson popped the metal cap from his beer. "So what happened, Barry?"

Barringer pushed out a rough, untamed sigh. "I came home yesterday, early, and caught her dragging a suitcase downstairs. Said she was leaving."

"What reason would Cali have to leave you, though?" Everson asked, seemingly confused. "I mean, women usually don't just leave, unless they've found someone else."

"Everson, I told you there is no one else." Barringer rubbed his hands across his head, thinking about that possibility – another man. The thought of another man touching his wife made his heart race with envy and rage.

"So why did she leave you, then, Gary?" Everson impatiently asked. "Stop keeping us in suspense and lay your cards out, man."

Lay your cards out...

Barringer leaned back in his chair, thinking about how he and Calista had made love yesterday afternoon. She was upset to the point of tears. Instead of sitting down and talking to her, all he could think to do was take her upstairs to the bedroom and make love to her. And something just occurred to him. While they were intimate, he told her he loved her. Twice he'd said it and neither time did she say it back.

Bryson looked at Barringer, really studied him to see if he would say it. Did he really *not* know why Calista left? Highly unlikely.

"Cali left because Barry wouldn't give her a baby," Bryson said, unable to bite his tongue any longer.

Barringer shot Bryson an incredulous stare. "How do you know she wants a baby?"

Bryson smirked. "She's only been asking, no *begging*, you for a baby since shortly after you married her. And you've been married for what? Five, going on six years now?"

Barringer buried his face in his hands.

"Listen, Barry, I've been so busy with Kalina, I didn't get a chance to have this conversation with you like I should have, but ah...you know Kalina owns a relationship blog called, The Cooper Files."

"I know."

"When I first met Kalina at Edith's Café, she was answering an anonymous email from a woman who sounded a lot like Calista. The woman had written in to the blog, asking if she should leave her husband since he wouldn't give her a baby."

Barringer sighed and shook his head. "Doesn't mean Calista wrote that."

"It doesn't, but I'm almost certain it was. Kalina thinks so, too."

"Okay, so let's say it was Calista. What did Kalina tell her to do? Leave me?"

"No."

"Then what?" Barringer asked, exasperated.

"It wasn't Kalina who answered the email, Barry. It was me."

"You?" Everson and Barry said together.

"Yeah. When I was helping Kalina with her work, that's what I was doing...answering emails. It's not like I wasn't qualified. I know a thing or two about relationships."

"Unbelievable," Barringer said. "So what did *you* tell Cali to do?"

Bryson thought about the email response he had typed:

It may be painful, but there is no reason why you should leave a man you love – a man that's been faithful to you, a man you married – because he's not ready to have a baby right now. Marriage is about making sacrifices. If you make this sacrifice for him, then surely, when the time is right whether it be two years or five years, he'll make the same sacrifice for you if the love and respect is mutual. Why don't you forgo the baby talk for now to help him chase his dreams? Let him know you're willing to put off having children a little while longer, but that you are serious about having a baby. Take it one day at a time. When the time is right, it will happen. Whatever you decide to do, please do not give him an ultimatum. Men hate those.

He looked at Barringer and said, "In the email, I told her she shouldn't leave a man she loved. Told her not to give you an ultimatum, to hang in there a little while longer and let you know how serious she was about having a baby. But I'm going to be honest with you, Barry. When I first read the email, it sounded like she was already leaning towards leaving. Sorry, man."

Bryson took a drink of beer.

"Here's the million-dollar question," Everson said. "Why not just give her a baby, Barry? Don't you want children?"

Barringer hung his head again. Giving her a baby would solve their problems, right? Wrong! Bringing a baby into a chaotic situation would only exacerbate their marital problems, not make them go away. But, baby talk aside, he had an even bigger problem...

Everson frowned. "Well?"

"I can't give her a baby," Barringer finally answered.

Everson's face twisted. "What do you mean you *can't*?"

"Yeah...can't or won't?" Bryson asked. "At some point, you have to weigh what's really important to you, Barry, and you can't keep putting your life, or her life, on hold while you stress out over Blackstone Financial."

"That's not what I'm doing."

"It's not?" Everson and Bryson asked together.

Barringer stood up, walked near the island and just stood there staring at his brothers for a moment before saying, "I haven't given her any children because I can't have children."

Bryson frowned. "What?"

"You heard me. I can't have children...not something a man wants to admit to, but there you have it. I can't have children...can't have a child of my own. So yes, I throw myself into

BFSG, expend all of my time, energy and efforts into making it a success, hoping I can do something right with my life, because the role of a father is one hat I will never wear."

"Barry, hold on," Bryson said, trying to wrap his mind around what his brother was saying.

The doorbell rang again.

Everson left the kitchen to answer it, inviting his cousin Rexford inside shortly thereafter.

"Hey, come on in Rex."

"What's up, man?" Rexford said. "Y'all didn't start the game without me, did you?"

"No." Everson rolled his wrist to check the time. "We got another hour and a half. You're early."

"Well, looks like Bryson and Barry are early, too," Rexford said, continuing on to the kitchen. "What's going down, fellas?"

"Hey, Rex," Bryson said.

Barringer didn't say a word. He just stood there, leaning against the island with his arms crossed.

"You cool, Barry?" Rex asked. "You over there looking like you done lost your best friend." Rexford chuckled.

"That's because he has," Bryson said.

Rexford dipped his head back and looked at the three men. "Crap...what did I just walk into?"

"Barry's having some issues and we're helping him iron them out," Everson said.

"So no card game?" Rexford asked.

"In about an hour, Rex. Grab a beer. There are some Doritos over there by the microwave,"

Everson said.

Bryson finally returned his attention to Barringer. "So when you say the role of a father is a hat you will never wear, what exactly do you mean?"

Barringer thought about it for a moment, unsure if he should let his brothers in on the secret he'd been carrying for years – one he tried to forget, but even with the demands of work, he couldn't fully brush it off. So after taking a breath, he looked at his brothers and said, "I can't be a father because I can't have children. I can't give Calista a baby because I—" Barringer shook his head. "I'm sterile. The chances of me impregnating a woman is less than one percent."

"What?" Bryson said.

"Man," Everson replied, not knowing what else to say.

"Okay, can somebody catch me up to speed on what's going on?" Rexford asked.

"No," Bryson and Everson said in unison.

Bryson followed up with, "You play too much, Rex, and this ain't a playing matter. Barringer is—"

"Calista left me," Barringer interrupted to say. He looked at Bryson and said, "He was going to find out eventually. No need to hide it."

"Calista left you?" Rexford asked with raised eyebrows. He knew how much Calista and Barringer loved each other and while he didn't believe in the institution of marriage, he saw how it worked well for other people. Well, there was Bryson's divorce from Felicia a few years back, but now Bryson was happily married to Kalina.

"Calista actually left you, Barry?" Rexford asked again in disbelief.

"Yeah."

"Packed bags and stuff?"

Barringer nodded. "When I got up this morning, she was gone."

"And she left you because you can't give her a baby?" Rexford asked.

"Yeah, but it's more complicated than that." Barringer scrubbed a hand down his mustache.

Everson shook his head. "I find it hard to believe that after you told Calista about your *problem*, she still decided to leave you," Everson said. "That's a slap in the face."

"Yeah," Rexford cosigned. "What ever happened to for better or for worse?"

Barringer grimaced and said, "It's not her fault. She doesn't know I'm sterile."

"You didn't tell her?" Bryson asked with raised brows above surprised eyes. "Barry, how could you not tell her?"

Barringer blew an agitated breath. "I couldn't tell her...couldn't get the words out. This isn't something I'm comfortable talking about."

"But she's your wife," Everson said. "If you can't confide in her, who can you confide in?"

"Guess that would be us," Rexford said offhandedly.

"Wait, fellas...something's not adding up," Bryson said. He looked Barringer square in the eyes and said, "Surely if you would've told Calista about your sterility, she'd be understanding. Calista's a good woman. She's not the type to bail for no reason. So tell us Barry, other than the fact that you know she'll be disappointed, and besides this issue causing you embarrassment, why would you not tell her?"

"Because I was afraid she'd ask me when I found out about it." Barringer rested his elbows on the countertop, covering his face with his hands. His back was to his brothers when he said, "I've known for a long time...known long before me and Calista were married, but I didn't tell her. I knew she wanted children. I promised her those children, but I couldn't tell her. I assumed I'd go through some therapy treatment...something that could fix me, and I tried for three of the five years we were married to *fix* myself but each and every time the doctor checked me, my count remained the same. I lied to her, and now, I'm paying for it."

Everyone was quiet. Too quiet.

"How about coming clean with her?" Bryson asked.

"Guess it doesn't matter now since she's already gone," Barringer said.

"It *does* matter if you want her back," Everson said.

Bryson stood up, walked over to his brother and pat him on the shoulder. "Come on Barry. You're not a quitter. Talk to her."

"That's going to be hard to do when I don't know where she is...when she won't answer her phone."

Bryson cocked his head to the side. "You have no idea where Calista could be right now?"

"No."

Bryson frowned, looked over at Everson then back to Barringer. "You have no idea?"

"No. Why do you keep asking me that? Do you have an idea? If so, enlighten me."

Bryson shook his head. How did Barringer not know the women were having a party for Vivienne? It was difficult to have his brother's back when he could clearly see why Calista left. In addition to the baby issue, he didn't take a personal interest in her. If he had, he would've known about the party. Calista surely wouldn't miss it.

"Everson," Bryson said, "Where's June right now?"

"At your house," Everson said.

"You see how Everson knew where his wife was."

"How's that helping me, Bryce, unless you're trying to tell me Calista is at your house, too?"

Bryson exhaled sharply.

"Is she?" Barringer asked impatiently.

"Kalina is hosting a party for Vivienne. The ladies are there now. Not sure if Calista is, but if I had to guess..."

"Then I'll see you guys later," Barringer said, heading for the door.

"Just don't go over there making a scene," Bryson told him. "Kalina spent a lot of time putting the party together for Vivienne. Don't ruin it."

And without replying to his brother, without saying another word to anyone, Barringer exited the front door.

"He really needs to take a step back from work," Bryson said. "It's taking too much out of him."

"I agree," Everson said, "But try telling him that. It's like talking to a brick wall."

"Well, somebody has to get through to him," Bryson said.

"Don't count on it. Now that he's lost a major account, he's really going to be cranky, working twenty-four-seven to get it back," Everson responded.

"The sad thing is, he probably wants the account more than he wants Calista," Bryson said.

"Now that was cold," Rexford said, pointing his bottle of beer towards Bryson.

"Well, he's headed to see her now. Maybe they'll work things out," Everson said, trying to remain optimistic.

"Yeah," Bryson said. "Maybe."

"Hey, where's Garrison these days?" Rexford asked.

Everson checked his watch. "He's probably on the way here. Unlike you fine gentlemen, Gary actually knows how to tell time."

Bryson grinned. "Sorry we infringed upon your two hours of wife-free time, Everson."

Everson turned up his beer, finishing it.

"I'm curious. What is it? You had plans or something?" Bryson asked.

"Wouldn't you like to know?" Everson said. "I'll get the chips and dip. Somebody call Gary and Colton to see if they're going to make it."

"I'm on it," Rexford said.

Chapter 7

Still sitting in her car and parked out in front of Kalina's house, Calista folded down the sun visor to look in the mirror, checking her eyes and makeup. She told herself not to cry anymore about her current situation, but the tears came anyway. When she married Barringer, she thought they'd be together forever. Even while she laid on the uncomfortable floor last night with her head perched up on towels, she tried to reconcile in her head how maybe she was doing this all wrong, acting on emotions and being irrational. Then she remembered what she'd given up for him. A family. A career. That's when the tears dried up. Nothing about her actions were unreasonable. Barringer was the unreasonable one.

She took a powder puff from her makeup bag, gently dabbing underneath her eyes. She had to get out of this car at some point, go inside and pretend to be happy so no one suspected anything was amiss. But how could she endure being around a very pregnant Vivienne while thinking about the child she never had, and probably never would have? She wouldn't admit this, but there were times she envied Vivienne and Garrison. Everything was going perfect for them. After being married two years, they were due to have their first child in a week or so.

Deciding to get out of the car before she talked herself into driving off, Calista grabbed her purse and headed for the door.

"It's Cali!" Candice said, opening the door before Calista had a chance to walk up the steps to the porch.

"Hi, Candy," Calista said, trying her best to plaster a smile on her face before she hugged her sister-in-law. "How are you?"

"I'm good. What about you?"

"I'm...okay," Calista said.

Candice picked up on her hesitancy. "Well, come on in."

Calista entered the house, feeling the weight of the world on her chest. Pretending to be happy when you were anything but was one of the hardest things for a woman to do. It was the ultimate act of not being true to one's self. A soul crusher. But today, Calista had to do that very thing. Fake it until the party was over.

She took off her shoes, left them at the door then pulled in a deep breath. *You can do this, Cali. You can do this. Forget about Barringer. Sit back, relax and have a good time.* She cleared her throat before walking into the family room bearing a bright smile – one which surprised her.

"Hey ladies," she said, walking over to hug Vivienne first.

Vivienne was comfortable, snuggled into the corner of the couch. Belly and all.

"Hey, Cali," June said, followed by Kalina.

Calista went to hug them both before finding a chair to settle into. On the table, she saw food and snacks. Her eyes roamed over everything.

"Cali, get a plate," Kalina said, "And help us eat this food. I made pizza bites, honey barbecue meatballs, fried shrimp, macaroni and cheese balls, brownies and there's more in the kitchen. I figured we'd start off with this first."

"Looks good," Calista said, taking a small saucer and helped herself to a sample of everything. Food would help her get through this night. She was starving since she hadn't had anything to eat today and if she was busy chewing, she wouldn't have to talk so much. Wouldn't have to think. Just eat.

"So, we were having some good ol' fashioned girl talk," Kalina said before she tossed a macaroni and cheese ball into her mouth.

"Yeah," June said. "Candice was getting ready to tell us about this handsome stud muffin I spotted her with."

Candice quirked up her lips. "Stud muffin?"

Vivienne laughed.

"What?" June asked with bright, playful eyes.

"Who says that anymore?" Candice asked jokingly. "Stud muffin..."

The women laughed together.

"He was muscular and cute," June explained. "Isn't that what a stud muffin is?"

"All right now," Vivienne said. "Don't let Everson hear you talking like that, June."

"Girl, please. Everson doesn't care. You know why?" June asked.

Vivienne finished chewing a meatball before she said, "Why?"

"Because he knows he's the ultimate stud muffin with his fine self."

"In that case, we're all married to stud muffins," Kalina said. "Our husbands look so much alike."

"And built like solid towers," Vivienne said.

"Sexy, chocolate towers," Kalina added. "See, now y'all got me checking my watch, waiting for my chocolate to get home."

"Ew," Candice said, faking a gag. One thing about hanging with the girls was, she had to sit through girl talk about her own brothers.

"Sorry, Candice," Kalina said on the back end of a laugh. "Keep forgetting you're the sister of these fine men."

Calista stuffed pizza bites inside of her mouth while forcing herself to grin.

"So finish telling us what happened, Candice," June said.

"Okay," Candice said, unfolding her legs and scooting to the very edge of the couch cushion. First of all, let me preference this story by saying, I was minding my own business at the Riverwalk."

Vivienne narrowed her eyes. "What were you doing at the Riverwalk by yourself, Miss Thang? You know that's couple central in Wilmington."

Candice shook her head. "Not really. That's a stereotype since it's a popular destination for couples, but I'm not going to stay away from the Riverwalk simply because I'm single. I want to enjoy my life. Since things ended with Quinton, I haven't even been looking for a man. Mom told me not to look. She said that's the problem with some women. They look for happiness in other people instead of finding it in themselves first."

"Amen," Kalina said.

All eyes focused on her.

"What?" Kalina asked. "I was happy before I met Bryce. I'm much happier with him, though."

"Aww…" Vivienne, June and Candice said together.

Calista tossed more food inside of her mouth.

"Anyway," Candice continued, "I decided to take my happy self down to the Riverwalk and enjoy some *me* time and out of nowhere, this guy, Kurt Hempstead, approaches me and hits me with the line, 'don't I know you from somewhere'."

"Oh, goodness," June said. "You would think men would try to come up with some new material."

"Why would they do that when the old

material works so well?" Kalina grinned.

"Plus, men are creatures of habit," Vivienne chimed in. "They are not changing anything unless they absolutely have to."

"That's true," Calista said. She finally found a place to jump in. Nearly six years with Barringer was all the proof she needed that men didn't change. They lied and told you what you wanted to hear just to shut you up for a little while and then it was back to the same old, same old.

"Wait, wait, wait, y'all," Kalina said. "I'm dying to know if Kurt Hempstead's one-liner worked on Candice."

"No, it didn't work on me. Short of rolling my eyes and telling him to get lost, I turned around and headed the opposite direction. That's when he asked me if I was related to Everson Blackstone."

June sat up tall. "He knew Everson?"

"Sure did. Said they went to high school together. So that's why you saw me talking to him, June. It's all Everson's fault." Candice took a sip of water.

"So who is this Kurt Hempstead? Tell us more," Vivienne said.

"Well, he said he lives in Asheville. He's a marketing manager at some company called TCC according to the business card he gave me."

June's brows arched. "He gave you his business card?"

"Yep, after he wrote his cell phone number on the back."

"Aw shucky ducky now," Kalina said.

"So are you going to see him again or what?" Vivienne asked.

Candice shrugged. "Not sure yet. I'm enjoying the single life." Candice ditched her water for a wine cooler.

"So in a couple of weeks, Theodore and Elowyn Blackstone are going to be proud grandparents," June said, switching up the conversation, looking at Vivienne.

"Girl, if they buy the baby anything else, Garrison and I will have to move into a bigger home," Vivienne said, then laughed.

"They're happy, though. I feel their excitement," Kalina said.

"What about you and Bryson?" Vivienne asked. "Will there be little Blackstones in your future?"

"Yes, in due time," Kalina said. "We're in no hurry. Right now, I selfishly want Bryson all to myself."

"Ew," Candice said. "Make it stop."

Kalina laughed. "Sorry, Candice."

"Me and Everson have been married for close to nine months," June said. "I know I'm not ready for a baby yet."

Vivienne looked at Calista, watching her eat. It just occurred to her that Calista had been especially quiet tonight, and this topic of conversation wasn't the best for her to chime in on. Everyone knew Calista wanted a baby and Barringer didn't want to give her one. He'd made all kind of excuses, saying he wasn't ready. Or the company needed him. Give him a year. That year would pass and he'd ask for another year.

"Calista, what's going on in your world?" June asked. "You're pretty quiet over there."

Calista shrugged. "Nothing much. These macaroni and cheese balls are the best, Kalina," she said, diverting.

"That's what I told her," Candice added, taking another one and tossing it inside of her mouth. "How's my care bear, by the way?" She asked, referring to Barringer, her nickname for him. "Things were pretty tense yesterday."

"Yeah, how is he doing? Garrison told me what happened," Vivienne said.

"Well, somebody fill me in," June said. "What happened?"

"Our biggest client signed on with one of our competitors," Candice explained. "Barringer took it hard. I tried to tell Barringer to chill...that there would be other big clients, but he was so angry, he packed up and left work early, and you know he *never* leaves early."

Calista knew that all too well.

"So how is Barry holding up, Calista?" Candice asked.

Calista shrugged and said, "Honestly, I don't know."

And then all eyes were on her...

Wearing a frown, Candice asked, "What do you mean you don't know?"

"Just what I said. I don't know," Calista shot back. She didn't mean to sound snippy. It just came out that way. The mere mention of Barringer's name incensed her.

"Did he not come home yesterday?" Candice inquired, sounding worried now.

Calista took a sip of her wine cooler before she said, "He came home. He was upset and—" Deciding not to hide her feelings or what was going on with her, she said, "I left Barringer."

"You did what!" the women shouted in one form or another.

"I couldn't take it anymore. I—" Tears slid down Calista's face.

Candice's eyes flashed concern. "When did you leave?"

Kalina walked over to Calista, kneeled down beside her and rubbed her back, trying to comfort her. "It's okay, Cali," she said.

Calista sniffled and dabbed her eyes with a napkin. "I left last night. I didn't want to leave him, I just...I couldn't lie to myself anymore. I want a family. He doesn't."

"But Barry has always wanted children," Candice said. "I think he's having problems prioritizing and with the demands of work and all—"

"No," Calista said, interrupting. "He does not want children. Otherwise, we would've had them by now."

"Where are you staying?" June asked.

"I have an apartment."

"An apartment?" Kalina asked. "So this wasn't a spur-of-the-moment thing."

"No, it wasn't."

"Wow," Vivienne said. "I can't believe it. Gosh, I thought you and Barringer would be together forever. I knew you weren't happy, but—"

"I was supposed to stay and be unhappy, right?" Calista interjected. "Was I supposed to keep my mouth shut and let him take me for granted, pretend we have the perfect marriage when, for years, I've known it was over?"

Candice swallowed hard, still in shock. "He just...just let you walk out? Just like that? Didn't try to stop you?"

"He *did* try to stop me, just like he stopped me the last few times I tried to leave him, but this time, I waited until he was asleep, got my suitcase and left."

"Oh my God," Candice said, burying her face in her hands. She loved Calista like a sister but Barringer was her brother, her real brother – her flesh and blood – and right now, she was worried about him. He looked like he was about to have a stroke when he left the office on Friday and now he had to deal with the fact that his wife left him.

The quick, back-to-back ringing of the doorbell interrupted the ladies.

Kalina stood up and walked to the door. Before she could get there, the bell rang more, followed by loud knocks. She wasn't expecting anyone else, so who was it at her door? She looked through the peephole to see Barringer standing there. *Crap*!

"Um, Calista, Barringer is here," she said after she'd swiftly walked back to the family room. The doorbell was steadily going off. "I'll tell him to leave if I have to, but I don't want to. Gosh, maybe I should tell Bryson to come handle this," she said, not knowing exactly what to do. She definitely didn't want to be in the middle of Calista and Barringer's marital problems.

She took out her cell, was going to dial Bryson when she saw a text from him:

Bryson: Not sure, but Barringer may be on the way over there. He hasn't been able to reach Calista by phone, so he wanted to see her in person. Long story.

That was one text message she'd read a little too late. She placed her phone on the table. "What should I tell him, Calista?"

Calista stood up and said, "Don't tell him anything. I'll go outside. I'm not going to drag you guys into our mess. And just so you know, I love all of you and I don't know how this will affect our relationships but I hope that no matter what happens, we can remain friends."

"We love you, too, Calista," they all said. Kalina, June and Candice hugged her.

Calista walked over to Vivienne, hugged her and said, "See you later, Viv." She gently touched Vivienne's stomach. "And I guess I'll be seeing you shortly, Junior."

With that, she headed for the door where she slid into her shoes. With her purse swinging from her shoulder, she opened the front door to a mean-faced Barringer Blackstone. The time had come to face the music.

Chapter 8

With tears clouding her vision, Calista swallowed the lump in her throat staring into Barringer's eyes. He actually looked hurt, but angry. Upon batting her eyes and blinking away tears, she realized she had it wrong. He looked more angry than he was hurt.

She stepped out onto the porch where he was standing, watching the porch light shine against his smooth, dark skin.

"So this is what you do to me?" he asked, with a raised voice, glaring at her. "This is what I'm worth to you?"

"You can stop yelling," she said calmer than she realized she would be.

"You make love to me then sneak out in the middle of the night like your life is so bad..."

"You must be mistaken. I didn't make love to you. I was just lying there while you did whatever it was you were doing in a lame attempt to get me to stay."

His face twisted in anger. "What?"

"Didn't work this time, Barringer."

He grinned, which she thought was out of place for the heated argument they were having. "You've got some nerve. This is how you talk to me. To your husband. After I break my back to provide for you, this is how you talk to me!"

"Stop yelling," she told him again.

"Don't tell me what to do!" he snapped, yelling louder with veins bulging out of his neck. "I'm talking to you. If you can sneak out of the house in the middle of the night like a teenager in heat, I can yell as loud as I want!"

"Then yell by yourself. I'm not going to listen to it. I'm done," she said, walking past him.

He grabbed her arm. "You're not done until I say you're done!"

"Let me go, Barry," she said, yanking her arm from his grasp, looking at him now. He must've lost his mind. He'd never grabbed her like that before. Never yelled at her like that before. He looked broken, like a man on the edge – still didn't change the fact that their marriage was over and had been for years. Did he really think yelling would encourage her to come back home?

"You have everything!" he yelled, veins engorged at his temples, "I give you everything! And this...this is how you repay me?" He turned his back to her and just as quickly turned around to face her again when he said, "I work from sun up to sun down to make sure you have everything you ever wanted in life—"

"I didn't ask you to do anything for me,

Barry. Well, I take that back. I did ask you, no I *begged* you to give me a family. That is the only thing I've ever asked of you," she said in tears now. "I never told you to take over your father's company, and—"

"Told me?" he said and dipped his head back. "You thought I needed your permission?"

"Not at all, but you could've talked to me about it. You decided to do it on your own...made the decision without even discussing it with me."

"That job takes care of us. That *job* has you living well...getting your hair and nails done...driving that Lexus *I* bought and paid for," he said pointing at her car. "You weren't complaining when I pulled up in the driveway with that."

She narrowed her eyes at him. "You are so full of yourself, Barry. I could've very well worked and made my own money, but you requested I didn't work. Said you wanted to be the breadwinner, and I was supposed to be a housewife. A mother." Calista chuckled amidst her tears and said, "But, I'm neither."

"What?" he asked, a frown growing deep in his forehead.

Calista wiped her eyes, sniffled and cleared her throat. With a shaky, distorted voice, she said, "It's a shame, really, that you think you can actually be a husband to me when you're married to your company. The company is your wife, not me. You eat breakfast, lunch and dinner there. Work so late, you may as well sleep there. You're with the company all the time, and you claim you're doing all of this work to take care of me? You're not taking care of me. I'm last place in your life, the position I've played for the last three...four years now and I'm not doing it anymore. I'll take care of myself from now on."

"Never knew you to be ungrateful, Calista," he said with flared nostrils.

"I'm not ungrateful."

"You are," he said, looking angrily at her. "I took care of you for five years and this is how you repay me?"

Calista could tell he was fighting back tears, but he wouldn't cry. He was too much of a man to cry. Too stuck on himself. Too right about everything. Too egotistical.

"Do you know how many women in this city wish they were you?" he asked.

Calista glared at him. *Did he really just ask me that?* What was this? A scare tactic? A way to get her to hold on to him so another woman couldn't have him?

"Don't look surprised," he said. "You *must* know you were lucky to end up with a man like me. A hard worker. A provider. Do you know how many women out there dream about the life you have, Cali?"

"I don't, but apparently you do, so go find those women and blow their heads up with false promises and lies. Tell them you'll give them the world, then turn around and throw it in their faces when they do something you don't like. Tell them to stay at home and take care of your invisible children, be a housewife, staring at walls all day long, cooking dinner for a man who never comes home. Who makes promises but doesn't keep any of them. They may fall for it, like I did in the beginning, but now, I know I deserve better. Go ahead and be some other woman's dream man, because you're no longer the man I dream about."

Barringer's jaw dropped.

"Goodbye, Barringer," she said, walking to her car.

"You won't find a better man than me!" he shouted behind her.

Calista rolled her eyes and continued on undeterred.

Chapter 9

Over the course of the next week, Calista managed to create some order in her life. She'd gotten a bed delivered, finally. She still hadn't purchased any living room furniture yet, deciding to use her savings wisely. The last thing she wanted to do was dip into the joint account she shared with Barringer. She needed money to live off of until she could find stable, steady employment. It was a good thing the job interview at the hospital went so well, she got offered the job on the spot. She was due to start working first thing Monday morning.

BARRINGER CALLED HER a few times, leaving angry messages, something about loyalty and betrayal, but he wouldn't be leaving anymore messages. Today, she officially turned off her old cell phone, threw it away and began using her new phone. She didn't have to tell anyone why she changed numbers. They knew why already.

When her new phone rang for the first time, she smiled when she saw who it was – Kalina. "Hello," she answered.

"Hey, you...haven't spoken to you since the party. How's it going? I see you have a new number."

Calista sighed. "Girl, it's been a rough week. Some days, I feel like I made a mistake. Other days I feel liberated, but sitting here now, I'm feeling like my stance hasn't accomplished much of anything. I'm still lonely."

"Are you up for some company on a Saturday night?"

"Um..." Calista said. She realized she hadn't given anyone her new address. That was intentional, a way to ensure Barringer didn't find out where she was staying. But she couldn't hide from the man forever. So she gave Kalina her address and awaited her arrival. She could use some company right about now.

* * *

"So this is my humble abode," Calista said. It wasn't until she said it that she realized how much house she'd given up for her tiny, little apartment. "I don't have living room furniture yet but we can sit on the bed. This way."

"Well at least you have a bed, girlfriend," Kalina said, toting a takeout bag towards the bedroom where Calista had been watching TV. "Bought you some fried chicken." She handed her the Styrofoam container.

"Thanks. I don't think I've eaten at all today."

"You don't *think*?" Kalina asked. "That's not good. I know things are pretty messed up right now, but you have to make sure you take care of yourself and your health."

"I know. You're right," Calista said. She took a bite of chicken and Kalina quietly started on her own meal.

"Hey, Cali, I have a question for you," she mumbled while eating.

"Okay."

"Did you, by any chance, send in an anonymous inquiry to *The Cooper Files* a while ago?"

Calista smirked. "I was wondering when you were going to make the connection. Yes, that was me. Little did I know the woman I was emailing would be my future sister-in-law. So embarrassing."

"You shouldn't feel embarrassed at all, Calista."

"But I do. I feel like this is my fault...like I'm somehow to blame for all of this, and since I'm the one who left him, the family, his family, blames *me* for breaking up our marriage. Doesn't matter what he did. They're all pointing fingers at me."

"Nobody's pointing fingers at you, and at this stage in the game, you can't be concerned about what everybody else thinks anyway.

Everybody else ain't living your life. They weren't in the house with you and Barringer. They don't know what stress you had to put up with. Now, with that being said, I can't take sides because I love you both. I'm new to the Blackstone family and the last thing I want to do is cause divisions among the people I love."

"I understand," Calista said.

"But I am open to talk about it, to be a listening ear."

"Do you remember when Barry showed up at your house the night we were having the party for Vivienne?"

"Yes. I wasn't being nosy, but I was looking out the window 'cause Barringer looked so angry, I didn't know what he was going to do. "

"He *was* angry...mad at me for leaving. I mean, I saw anger blazing in his eyes and you know what the sad part is, Kalina?"

"What's that?"

"I haven't seen him express feelings so genuine since our honeymoon. The other day, he was so mad, I could feel it, just like I could feel how much he loved me the night of our honeymoon. He didn't have to touch me or anything. All I did was look into his eyes and I...I felt it."

"Wow. Well, I don't know Barringer that well, but from what I can tell, he seems like a pretty nice guy."

"He was a lot nicer in the beginning. Now, he's irritable and cranky. Yet and still, I love him." Calista sighed. "I held up my end of our marriage. He didn't return the favor. All I wanted was a family and for him to dedicate as much time to me as he does to his work. That's all I wanted. But he wanted to give me *things* – necklaces and handbags – like all that stuff was going to make me happy. I didn't ask to move to that big house we live in. I was fine with the much smaller house. I didn't ask him to buy me a Lexus. He did it because he wanted to, and while it's nice, it's just a *thing*. I don't love it. I can't make a baby with a car, can I?" Calista laughed.

Kalina giggled, tickled to tears.

"Overall, he's a good man, and yes, he will give me anything I want when it comes to material things, but what about when I need him to hold me at night and he's still at the office? As I sit here talking to you, I'm remembering all the nights I went to bed alone. All the times I cooked dinner for us, only for him to tell me he wasn't going to make it home."

"Have you thought about counseling?"

"I have, but Barringer won't have time for counseling. He has made it clear that his job is more important than I'll ever be."

"Have you *asked* him to go to counseling with you?"

"No."

"Then maybe you should ask."

Calista shook her head. "No. I can't. It's too late now."

"It's never too late when you love someone, Calista."

"It is, because no matter how much I love

him, he still doesn't love me enough to value me. Another man..." She paused. The thought of being with another man made her breath catch. Made her stomach ache. She was starting over, yes, wanted a man who wanted the same things she wanted, yes, but the thought of being with another man, besides Barringer, made her sick.

"What were you saying? About another man?" Kalina asked. She narrowed her eyes and asked in a low tone, "There isn't another man, is there?"

"No. Of course not. What I was going to say was, I could find another man who wanted the same things I wanted, but I don't want another man. I want *my* man. The thought of being with someone else other than Barringer makes my skin crawl," Calista said. Her body wiggled like she was instantly struck with a chill.

Kalina giggled. "Sorry for laughing, but it's so clear to me you're still in love with him. Maybe this time apart is what you need. Now that Barringer knows how important these issues are to you, maybe he'll actually address them instead of brushing them off."

"Let's hope so. Otherwise, it'll just be me and my little apartment."

"Yep. You and your apartment."

"How's Vivienne doing, by the way? I meant to call her, but I got sidetracked."

"I saw her the other day, briefly. She didn't look too good. Looks like she's retaining a lot of fluid."

"Oh."

"She didn't seem like she was in any pain, though."

"Okay. I'll try to call her tomorrow before I start working."

"Working? You got a job, Calista?"

"Yes. This past Wednesday, I interviewed for a position in the outpatient department at Regional. They offered me the job the same day."

"That's wonderful."

"Yeah," Calista said, downcast, because working and providing for herself would make it seem like her split from Barringer was permanent. She hated that feeling.

"Anyway, I have to get going," Kalina said standing. "Bryce and I are going to catch a movie."

"Okay."

"See you later, sis," she told Calista.

"Okay. Later. Oh, and thanks for the food."

"You're welcome."

"And thanks for thinking about me. I know you took time away from Bryson to come here which is partly the reason I didn't want you to come by, at first. Now, I'm glad you did. I really appreciate it, Kalina."

"Anytime, Cali."

When Kalina exited, Calista stood behind the door and sighed. A large bucket of extra butter popcorn and a movie sounded good right about now. She couldn't remember the last time Barringer took her to a movie.

She expelled a breath. Looked like she would have to settle for a TV movie, microwave popcorn and a blanket instead.

Chapter 10

Calista didn't think it would be difficult to settle into a new work environment, but it was somewhat overwhelming – being introduced to so many people. Since the director of the unit was out of town attending a conference, Shavonda, one of the administrators, showed Calista around and gave her a brief overview of the outpatient department.

Now, Calista was exhausted. As soon as she returned to her office, she buried her face in her hands, sighed heavily and kicked off her heels. After a few deep breaths, she called Vivienne to confirm their lunch plans for the day.

"Hi, Cali," she answered.

"Hey, Viv. How are you?"

"Feeling a tad bit better," Vivienne said. "We're still meeting for lunch, right?"

"Yes. That's why I was calling...wanted to make sure you were still up for it."

"I wouldn't miss it for the world."

Wouldn't miss it for the world? Calista thought Vivienne's choice of words was a little strange. "Okay, then I'll see you in about twenty minutes."

"Okay."

Calista hung up the phone and said out loud, "Wouldn't miss it for the world...why would she say that?"

Figuring she was reading too much into it, she stood up, stepped back into her shoes, preparing to go when Shavonda tapped lightly on her opened door to get her attention.

"Hey, Shavonda."

"Hey, Calista. Thought I'd check in to see how the morning has been so far."

"So far, so good."

"Yeah, I doubt it'll take you a long time to pick up on the swing of things around here."

"I sure hope not, though, I have to say I don't have a thing to be worried about. Looks like there's a great bunch working here."

"The best," Shavonda replied, glancing around the office. "Anyway, enjoy your lunch."

"Thank you. I'll be back at around 1:30 p.m."

"Okay."

"Oh, and make sure you savor your lunch hours," Shavonda said. "You'll realize the importance of lunch breaks when you really get into the thick of things."

"Duly noted," Calista said, smiling.

* * *

Calista tried not to look too shocked when she saw Vivienne sitting at a table in the Mexican restaurant. Kalina was right. Vivienne's face was swollen, along with her arms and hands. It had only been a week since they last saw each other. What happened? Did she drive herself here? Take a taxi? Did Garrison drop her off?

"Hey you," Calista said, finally close enough to the table.

"Hey, Calista," Vivienne said, lifting her head high enough so Calista could hug her.

Calista took a seat and said, "I have to say I was surprised you wanted to leave the comforts of your home to come out here. It's all wet and dreary today and you'll be having the baby in less than a week."

"I know," Vivienne said, rubbing her stomach. "And I wouldn't have come out if it wasn't urgent that I met with you."

Calista's head flinched back. "Urgent? What's going on, Vivienne?"

Vivienne smiled warmly. "Well, I wanted you to know that even though you don't have a child, I think you would make an excellent mother. I know you will."

"Thank you, Vivienne, but I don't understand what that has to do with your reason for asking me to lunch. You're kinda freaking me out."

Tears came to Vivienne's eyes. "Listen, Calista...um, there's no easy way for me to say this, so here goes. "I want you to be a mother to my son, because I—" Her voice cracked. "I won't be able to." Tears spilled from her eyes.

"Vivienne, you're scaring me," Calista said, touching Vivienne's trembling hand.

Somehow, through her sadness, Vivienne managed to talk. "I don't know why I'm crying. I've already accepted this."

"Accepted what?"

"That I won't survive the birth of my son."

"Viv—"

"Just listen to me for a minute, Cali. Please."

When the waitress came over to take their food orders, both women decided on water. Neither could eat.

Vivienne took a breath when the waitress walked away then continued, "The doctor informed Garrison and I, four months ago, that the likelihood I would survive the birth of the baby was low. I've been struggling with eclampsia the entire pregnancy and...well the doctor told me to terminate the pregnancy. I couldn't do that. I wouldn't do it. It was difficult for me and Garrison but, ultimately, I know I'm doing the right thing." She wiped tears from her face. "I want my son to live...want him to have a chance at life. I've had my life. It's his turn now."

"No," Calista said, her eyes glistening with tears.

"Cali—"

"Doctors are not perfect. They're not God. They don't know what's going to happen."

"They're not perfect, but listen to me, Cali. Look at my face. It's swollen. My hands are swollen. I have constant headaches...headaches so severe, it makes it hard for me to see sometimes. Garrison had to drive me here to meet you."

"No," Calista said with trembling lips. "This can't be happening."

"I need you to promise me, Calista. Promise me you'll take care of my baby."

Calista frowned again. "Vivienne—"

"Garrison won't be able to do it all on his own. He's having a hard enough time coming to grips with this as it is."

This can't be happening, Calista thought as she smeared tears away from her eyes. The last time she saw Garrison, he looked fine, like everything was okay. Well, so did Vivienne, so maybe that didn't mean much. But Garrison – she knew him better than the family was aware, especially since they'd dated for a year a half back in college. Originally from Raleigh, North Carolina, Calista had moved to Wilmington to attend college where she met Garrison. They were the same age, had a lot in common, but she broke up with him when she felt the relationship wasn't going anywhere. She never told anyone about their college courtship and Garrison thought it was best not to mention anything to Vivienne about it, but given the circumstances, Calista didn't feel like she had much of a choice. She had to tell Vivienne now.

"Have you spoken with Garrison about this?"

"I have."

"And he agreed I should do this?"

"He did."

"Then you need to know that—"

"I know. You and Garrison dated back in college. He told me."

Calista's sad eyes grew big. "He told you?"

"Yes, a few months ago when we first started discussing the possibility of you taking care of the baby. Will you do it?"

Calista wiped her eyes again. "I don't want to accept what you're telling me, Vivienne. We can't lose you. This isn't right."

"It's not right, but it's...it's reality. Please promise me you'll take care of Junior."

"Yes, I'll take care of him," Calista said absently. "Who else knows about this, Vivienne?"

"My doctor knows. Garrison knows. I know and now, you know."

"This can't be real," Calista said, holding her throbbing temples. "It can't be."

"It is. I know how much you want a baby...how much you want to be a mother. Well, now, you...you finally get to be a mother," Vivienne said. She began crying.

Calista reached across the table to hold Vivienne's hand. This was really happening. Vivienne thought she was going to die and was asking her to take care of the baby. For a moment, Calista thought her sister-in-law was paranoid, but Vivienne was anything but. She was always the planner out of the Blackstone women – the one who liked order. Who'd plan vacations, even trips to the grocery store down to the last detail. True to character, she was proactively making plans for her child in the event she didn't survive childbirth. A true mother, she wanted a guarantee that her son would be loved and cared for. She was hoping for the best but preparing for the worst.

Still, Calista couldn't help but feel like this wasn't reality. She'd always considered Vivienne and Garrison to be the perfect couple, not one of those happy-in-public couples (like she and Barringer), but a real couple who genuinely loved each other. She could see that love at their many family dinners, vacations and other random get-togethers. She could see it when they'd gotten married.

Garrison had given the most beautiful vows she'd ever heard, the kind of vows that made women *ooh* and *ah*, wishing they had a man who could be so authentically sweet and thoughtful. Vivienne had him. How could something like this disrupt their happily ever after?

"Listen, Calista, I don't want you to feel sorry for me. I made this decision. I'm okay with it. I'm sad, yes, but at peace and I will always be as long as I know you will be there for my son."

Calista closed her eyes, pushing out tears in the process. The doctor had this one wrong. Vivienne would be fine and have a beautiful, healthy baby boy. Life would go on as normal and this conversation would be a forgotten memory. But in case that's not how things ended up, she opened her eyes, looked at Vivienne and said, "I will take care of Junior and love him just like you would. I love you,

Vivienne."

"Love you, too, sis, and thank you. I know this is a lot to ask and I appreciate it very much."

The women dried their eyes as best as they could. Afterwards, Calista proceeded to help Vivienne to the car.

WHEN HE SAW the women approaching, Garrison got out of the car, opened the passenger door and helped Vivienne get inside. After closing the door, he looked at Calista with a set of worried eyes.

"Everything is going to be okay, right?" Calista asked him.

He grimaced before saying, "Just pray for us." He walked away from her and settled back inside the car.

Calista waved at Vivienne before heading to her car where she got in and cried harder. Even though Vivienne had plainly explained everything to her, she couldn't wrap her mind around this. And how was she going to return to work with a red nose and puffy eyes?

She quickly dug around in her purse for powder foundation and eye drops. She had to make it through another four hours of work before she could go home and completely fall apart.

Chapter 11

Barringer sat upright at his cherry-oak desk, beyond frustrated. After taking two unplanned days off work, Thursday and Friday of last week, in addition to Saturday and Sunday, he failed at getting himself in the right frame of mind for work. Failed miserably. Suddenly, work didn't seem important. Well, it was still important, but with the chaos in his life, his focus waned.

And now he was sitting at his desk, Monday morning, with his arms crossed while staring at the computer screen. He rubbed his eyes. Work? How could he work like this? He couldn't do a thing. Couldn't think straight.

He rubbed his eyes again.

He had no desire to attend the conference call he was supposed to be on right now, nor did he have the motivation to type a response to the email from Eleanor, his administrative assistant – the email he'd been staring at for the last ten minutes. He didn't read it. Just stared at the bright screen, seeing characters, letters, words, but he hadn't read anything. All he could think about was Calista.

What was she doing right now? Was she thinking about him? Was he that bad of a husband – so awful she had to leave? No talking it out? No second chance? No nothing?

His wandering thoughts were interrupted by the ringing of his desk phone. He glanced at the display, saw Candice's extension, but he hadn't bothered to answer. Instead, he looked at the computer screen and decided to make a real attempt at work:

FROM: Eleanor Hargrove
TO: Barringer Blackstone
CC: Candice Blackstone; Garrison Blackstone
SUBJECT: Possible New Account – Telmark Corp.

Barringer,

I'm attaching an email I received from Telmark Corporation. They're hoping to meet with you soon. Let me know if you would like for me to put a meeting on the calendar.

Thanks,
--
Eleanor Hargrove | Administrative Assistant to Barringer Blackstone
Blackstone Financial Services Group (BFSG)
Ext. 217

Telmark Corporation...

Barringer leaned back in his chair and suspired. Blackstone Financial could use a new account after the loss of Blakeney, no matter how big or small, but when his mind was consumed with thoughts of Calista, how was he supposed to concentrate on a new account? He thought she'd come to her senses and come back home, especially after he found out she'd been living in a one-bedroom apartment – rags compared to the riches he'd given her. She must've been too prideful to use money from their joint account because she hadn't used the debit card or made any withdrawals. He was certain she'd been using her personal savings, and then he found out she'd gotten a job – a managerial role at Regional Hospital. She actually got a job. His wife was supporting herself. If she was working to support herself, she wouldn't need him, would she? Obtaining a job was an act of independence. She was saying a lot without actually saying anything, but he got the message loud and clear. She didn't need him. Not anymore.

Since she'd gotten a new phone number – a number he wasn't privy to, he thought about calling the hospital and asking to speak with her or maybe he'd show up out of the blue, talk some sense into her because apparently she'd lost her mind.

The knock at the door took him out of his thoughts. Barringer glanced up and saw Garrison peeping around the door.

"Got a minute?" Garrison asked.

"Come in," Barringer mumbled, wishing he'd locked his door. He wasn't in the mood for this – conversations about work. He was too busy thinking about Calista to work.

Garrison walked in and took a seat in one of the leather chairs in front of his brother's desk. He gave Barringer a hard lingering look.

Barringer expelled a breath. "Are you just going to sit there, or did you want something?"

"Whoa, Barry...chill, man. Whatever it is you're going through, it's not the end of the world. Trust me."

"Oh, don't try to pretend you have no idea what I'm going through. I'm certain Bryson and Everson have filled you in on the current events of my life since you weren't at Everson's house last Saturday. Where were you anyway?"

"Home. I wasn't in the mood for playing cards and I didn't want to ruin it for the rest of y'all, so I stayed home."

"Well, you definitely wouldn't have ruined it. I single handedly did that by talking about Calista. Then I left early and didn't go back."

"Why didn't you go back?" Garrison asked, though he knew the answer. Vivienne had already filled him in on Calista's tearful confession that night at the party. He knew Calista had left his brother.

Barringer released a frustrated sigh. "Calista left me, man. She actually left *me*."

"You say that like it's impossible for a woman to leave you."

"It is," he replied in an arrogant tone.

"Before I married Calista, you think I was the type to sweat a woman. Not at all, bruh. *I* broke off relationships. *I* ended things. No woman has ever walked out on me."

"But Calista."

Barringer narrowed his eyes at his brother. "Obviously."

"Barry, I didn't say that to be a jerk."

"Then why'd you say it, Gary?"

"Just stating facts. To me, it seems like instead of focusing on the reason Calista left you, you're more worried about your ego."

Barringer's eyes darted towards his younger brother. He was only two years older than Garrison, but everyone thought of Garrison as the next oldest, to Bryson that is, because of his mild, laid back demeanor. Barringer, who was actually the next oldest to Bryson, was anything but. He was the overachiever, the one who had to be in charge, which is why he had stipulated, before they married, Calista not work outside of the home. He couldn't necessarily be king of the castle if his queen was seen around town fending for herself, now could he?

His forehead creased when he said, "Then tell me, Gary, since you think you have all the answers—"

"I don't have all the answers, Barry," Garrison interrupted.

"You said I was worried about my ego, so tell me what you would do if you were me. What would you do if Vivienne left you?"

Garrison leaned back in his chair. If the doctors were right, Vivienne *was* leaving him.

Permanently. Calista knew about it, but other than her, he'd kept this to himself – kept it a secret from his brothers, his sister and his parents, and he had intended on keeping it to himself right down until the end, hoping the doctors were wrong.

Garrison pulled in a breath, suppressed sadness and looked up at Barringer. "Well, I love my wife, so I would do everything in my power to get her back."

Barringer's eyes flashed atomic heat. "Are you implying I don't love Calista?"

"Not at all, Barry. You asked me what I would do if Vivienne left me and I simply said I love her and would do everything in my power to get her back. Would you be willing to do that with Calista? Or are you going to allow pride to keep you two apart?"

Barringer didn't respond.

"And let's not forget you lied to her," Garrison continued. "You led her to believe you wanted children. I was surprised to hear you couldn't have any."

Barringer stood up and paced the floor with his hands in his pockets.

"Listen, Barry...I know it must be difficult—"

"Actually, you don't know," Barringer snapped, "Because, last I checked, Vivienne is due to give birth to your child at any moment now. A son."

"Yes, but—"

"I can never have that! So you don't know how I feel," Barringer erupted. "I can't give my wife a child and I'll never be able to carry on my legacy. I can't have a son of my own. You *have* a son. I'll never have that!"

"Okay, I'm sorry if—"

"Save it, Gary! I don't need your apology."

Garrison stood up, preparing to leave. Barringer was too incensed to talk or think rationally. His brother's temper got the best of him at times and with the added pressure of losing a major account around the same time he lost his wife, his temper was even worse. "Just communicate with your wife," Garrison told him.

"And say what. Oh, baby I love you, but I'm a loser. I can't give you a baby."

Garrison rubbed his hand across his forehead, growing more frustrated by the minute. "I'm going to go back to my office. I'll talk to you later." Garrison was steps away from the door when he heard Barringer say:

"I tried hormone treatments for two years. Two. Every time the doctors re-checked my count, it remained unchanged. I wanted to give Calista a baby. Wanted us to have the perfect family like you and Vivienne. Unfortunately, things didn't work out that way."

"Be honest with her, man. You have to tell her."

"Why? To give her more ammunition to divorce me?"

Garrison's brows snapped together. "Divorce? Who said anything about divorce?"

"Calista moved out. Isn't divorce the next step?" Barringer sat down again, burying his face in his hands. He moved them away then said, "Anyway, what did you want? You must be here for some reason."

"It's…it's not important. I'll talk to you about it later."

"About what?"

Garrison didn't want to talk about anything related to the baby after Barringer's blow up, but since he insisted, he said, "I told you I was taking some time off."

"As you should with the baby coming and all."

"Well, I've decided not to come back."

Barringer could only shake his head.

"I'll try my hardest to help my replacement transition into this role as smoothly as possible," Garrison said.

"I imagine you've already spoken with Dad about this," Barringer said.

"No, I haven't. Dad doesn't run this company any more. You do."

"But he founded this company and with you gone, I'm going to be the only one of his sons working here." He chuckled uncomfortably. "This is great. Just what I need. First, I lose a multi-million dollar account, then my wife leaves me, now my brother is quitting on me."

"Barry, everything is not about you."

"You're right. It's about everyone else screwing me over. But, hey, that's life, right? It works for some people and for others, it sucks."

Garrison shook his head. "In the grand scheme of things, you don't know how good you got it, man, so why don't you stop this pity party you're having and learn to appreciate what you have."

"I do appreciate what I have."

"No, you don't," Garrison said firmly, "Because if you did, Calista would have never left you. You can try to make her the villain in all of this, but the truth of the matter is, you didn't hold up your end of the marriage and you have no one to blame but yourself."

Barringer's brows furrowed. "You don't know nothing about my marriage."

"I know you don't have one at the moment, and until you realize your role in her leaving you, you'll always find a reason to blame other people for your mistakes. I'm out."

"Be out, then!" Barringer yelled from behind his desk.

As Garrison exited the office, Barringer's desk phone rang. Candice was calling again. Barringer took a breath, attempting to calm himself down before he picked it up.

He failed.

"What is it, Candice?"

"Hey, did you see the email from Eleanor."

"I get tons of emails from Eleanor. Can you be more specific?"

"The one about Telmark. It's a possible new account for us. I think we need to set up a meeting right away. They're not as big as Blakeney, but hey, at this point, we need to take what we can get."

"Then set up the meeting. I'm occupied with other things at the moment. I don't have time for a new account."

"Barringer, it would be rude for you not to

be available to meet with their CEO."

"I didn't say I wouldn't meet with the CEO. I said, set up the meeting, Candice. You want to set it up, set it up!"

"Okay, jeez. I'll set it up," Candice said with a raised voice.

Was everybody trying to give him attitude today? He could give it right back. "Where was this dedication to The Blakeney Agency?"

"Excuse me."

"You heard me. You're the customer relations manager and you let Blakeney slip right through the cracks."

"Wait a minute...*I* let them slip away? I told you three months before Blakeney signed with another company that they were fishing. As I recall, you blew it off like I didn't know what I was talking about while you looked for new business. So don't try to turn this around on me, Barry."

"I don't have time for this. If you want to set up a meeting, set it up. If you don't, don't. I can't even do my own job right now. How on earth am I supposed to do yours?"

"I'm not asking you to do my job, Barry."

"Sure sounds like it."

"You're being a real jerk right now."

"Yeah, well this *jerk* has work to do. Bye." Barringer hung up the phone and sighed heavily again. He had to get himself together. So far, he hadn't done one productive thing today. Deciding to start with replying to Eleanor's email, he responded:

FROM: Barringer Blackstone
TO: Eleanor Hargrove
CC: Candice Blackstone; Garrison Blackstone
SUBJECT: Re: Possible New Account – Telmark Corp.

Eleanor,

Candice will be taking the lead on this account. Please direct future correspondence directly to her.

Thanks,
--
Barringer Blackstone | CEO
Blackstone Financial Services Group (BFSG)
Ext. 200

———

Chapter 12

"Don't go in there, girl. Oh my God! Stop!" Calista yelled, sitting in the middle of her bed, in the dark, tossing cheddar cheese popcorn inside of her mouth while her eyes were pinned to the TV. "Don't do it. Don't do it!" She was watching a movie about a woman whose new next door neighbor, a man, was stalking her. Only thing was, this woman didn't know it. Now, her stalker had her in a chokehold while holding a rag drenched in chloroform over her nose.

"Told you not to go in there, stupid," Calista mumbled with a mouthful of popcorn. "Now you're going to be chained in this maniac's basement."

Her attention shifted from the TV to her cell phone vibrating on the bed. Kalina's number was on the display. "Hey, Kalina," she answered.

"Are you on the way?"

Calista frowned. "On the way where?"

"To the hospital. Garrison called and said Vivienne's being induced today. Don't know why she had to be taken by ambulance, though, but at any rate, the baby is going to be here soon. I'm so excited!"

Calista's heartbeats pounded in her chest like drums. "Okay. I'm on the way."

Calista jumped off the bed, took off her pajamas and slid into the pair of jeans she'd left on the floor next to the bed. And when she was able to put on a bra, a T-shirt and grab a jacket for the chilly night, she stepped into a pair of slip-on canvas shoes, snatched her purse from the kitchen counter and ran out the door.

* * *

When she arrived at the hospital, the Blackstone family had taken over the maternity waiting room. Elowyn trembled with excitement as she sat next to her husband Theodore. Candice sat on the other side of her mother, checking her timeline on her phone. Everson leaned in closer to Bryson chatting it up about something sports-related. June and Kalina seemed busy with their own conversation.

After speaking to everyone and hugging Elowyn and Theodore (she hadn't seen her in-laws in a while), Calista sat down, not directly among the family but near them, saying silent prayers for Vivienne. Too bad the rest of the family didn't know. Vivienne and Garrison could use all the prayers they could get. They all should've been praying instead of talking about football, checking social media and cackling about some stupid reality TV show.

Calista sighed. She threaded her fingers together, rested her chin on top and closed her eyes. She would have to pray enough for everybody. She hoped the doctors were wrong and Vivienne, and the baby, made it safely through labor. A child needed its mother – its *real* mother – and while she would fulfill her promise to Vivienne if it came down to it, she could never completely fill Vivienne's shoes. No one could.

Calista blew a breath of frustration that was loud enough to catch Elowyn's attention. She smiled warmly at her mother-in-law and rubbed her eyes while feeling a dark aura near her. She didn't have to lay eyes on this *being* to know it was Barringer. She smelled his cologne, his scent and for a reason she couldn't explain, the smell of him made tingles run through her. Made her cheeks rosy. She hadn't seen him in ten days. Now he was here, sitting in the chair next to her. Not a chair away or across from her. Next to her. And he didn't say a word. Just sat there. Was this some sort of intimidation?

Calista released a pent up breath, looked up and saw Kalina and June staring at her. She could imagine what they must've been thinking. She saw Candice look at Barringer and rolled her eyes while shaking her head.

Calista wouldn't look at him. She avoided him, refused to be the first one to say anything, and while they sat quietly she could feel his eyes on her. He was recording every inch of her face, her hair, lingered at her lips, before his eyes rolled down her arms to her hand.

"I see you're not wearing the five-thousand-dollar ring I bought you," Barringer said when he noticed she wasn't wearing her wedding ring.

Calista glanced at her left hand. No, she wasn't wearing the ring. There was no need to wear it. A ring that once meant something, a symbol of his love, was now a reminder of a marriage she no longer wanted to be a part of.

"Guess it doesn't mean anything, anymore, huh?" Barringer asked with a hint of disappointment in his voice.

Calista turned to look at him for the first time. He looked rough, not in a bad way but a bad boy type of way. She wondered when he'd last shaved. And he had on a suit. Must've came straight from the office. Typical. Nothing had changed about his routine. He was still working well into the night.

Looking him in the eyes, Calista responded, "Now is not the time nor the place to discuss this. I'm here for Vivienne." She turned her attention away from him, rested her elbows on her knees again, closed her eyes and began saying another prayer for Vivienne.

Barringer leaned close to her ear and whispered, "It's funny how you can be there for everyone except me."

"Barry—"

"And changing your number," he let out a

snide grin. "That was real mature of you, Calista."

"Like it was mature of you to leave me ten voicemails and twenty text messages in one night. Yeah, *real* mature."

"You left me," he said angrily. "I left those messages to get your attention."

Calista couldn't help the grin that escaped her lips. "Oh, is that how it works? You wait until I leave and *then* you try to get my attention. Brilliant," she said in a sarcastic tone.

"You had my attention before."

"No, I didn't. Your job had your attention. Still does."

"That's a lie."

"It's not a lie. Your job is the most important thing in your life. Look at you...you're dressed up right now. It's ten o'clock and you still have on a suit. I know you just came from the office, but now, I don't care. You can work twenty-four hours a day without having to hear me nag, whine and complain anymore that you work too much. That should make you happy."

Barringer rubbed the back of his neck. "You know what would make me happy? A wife who appreciates me, who appreciates everything I've done for her," he said through gritted teeth.

"Then good luck finding one, Barringer."

A deep frown appeared in his forehead. "What are you saying, Calista? Are you saying it's over between us?"

Calista looked at him for a long moment.

Choosing her words carefully she said, "I'm not happy when I'm with you. Face it, Barringer. We grew apart. You have your work, and I have...well I have nothing. I know you're angry with me, and that's fine. Be angry. I was angry for years but that didn't change anything, did it? I was still Calista Blackstone, Barringer's wife. That's all people know me for...being your wife like that's a job title or something. *Barringer's wife*. And I was barely even a wife to you. You stayed gone and I don't know if it was intentional. I tried to think it wasn't...tried to reason in my head that you were trying to be *the* man by working hard to provide for your household, but then I got to thinking...why is he working so hard when it's only me and him? When we share a five-bedroom house that's so cold and empty, I can hear my own echo. And who are you supporting? Me? Because I never asked to be supported. You volunteered. Told me you wanted to be the breadwinner, so I let you win bread while I did absolutely nothing with my degree."

"You agreed—"

"I know what I agreed to. That's why I stayed home and did the Susie Homemaker thing – cooked for you, paid bills, did housework – well things the cleaning agency wouldn't do. But it was just me, always at home. Alone. Working. And you, Barringer Blackstone were never there." Calista dabbed her eyes. "It was just me and the house. And the TV, but never you. I was lonely, and I still am. I'm lonely, but the only difference is, now I don't have any expectations. When I go to my apartment, I know it'll just be me, and I'm okay with that."

Calista stood up with the intention of finding a bathroom but first, she turned to Barringer and said, "When you walked in and sat next to me, I sensed your presence. I smelled your cologne and it gave me goosebumps. You haven't given me goosebumps in years, but I felt it a few minutes ago and it proves to me that I still love you. I will always love you, Barry, and I'm sorry we've become a statistic...sorry our marriage...didn't...didn't work."

Calista continued on to the bathroom.

Barringer rubbed his face and sighed deeply before noticing all eyes were on him. But the eyes of his parents were much more inquisitive than everyone else's, and rightly so. Before tonight, they had no idea he and Calista were having problems.

Barringer hung his head. He should've listened to Calista when she told him now wasn't the time nor the place to talk about their personal business. Instead of everyone focusing on welcoming the newest addition to the Blackstone family, they'd be thinking about the latest subtraction – Calista.

Elowyn stood up, walked over to Barringer and took the seat Calista had been sitting in. "What was that about, Barringer?"

"Nothing, Mother," he said, running his palm across his mother's full head of gray hair. The last thing he wanted was for her to worry.

"It didn't look like nothing to me, son."

"Me and Calista are going through some things right now. I'll talk to you about it later, okay. For right now, let's focus on Gary and Viv."

Chapter 13

Garrison came out into the waiting area in a blue gown, blue booties covering his shoes and a bonnet on his head.

Everyone rose to their feet in excitement.

Around the same time, Calista stepped back inside the waiting area, looking at Garrison, seeing something no one else saw. Worry. No one knew to look for it, so how could they see it?

"Well?" Everson said. "Do we have a nephew yet?"

"Ah..." Garrison swallowed the lump in his throat. "He's here. He's seven pounds, two ounces...twenty-one inches long."

Cheers erupted. Claps. Celebratory hugs.

Candice wrapped her arms around Garrison. "Congratulations, Gary. I'm so happy!"

Gary forced himself to smile.

"How's Viv?" Kalina asked.

"Yeah, how's Vivienne?" June said.

Garrison's lips trembled. "Um…"

Candice frowned. "Gary, what's wrong?"

"Vivienne's not doing all that great," he said, his voice strained.

"What do you mean?" Theodore asked.

Garrison glanced up and locked eyes with Calista. Looking at his father again, he said, "She's in a coma."

Tears dropped from Calista's eyes as she walked back down the hallway, near the bathrooms. Using the wall for support, she cried while hiding her face behind her hands.

"No," Candice said, her hand over her heart. "What happened?"

Garrison went on to explain how, from the start, the pregnancy was high-risk for Vivienne and they'd known all along this could happen. He told them it's what Vivienne wanted. She wanted to give him a son…wanted their baby to live.

"The doctors don't think she'll make it through the night," Garrison said before he completely broke down and cried. Bryson held him up while Candice tried to console him. Barringer and Everson went to stand by their brother's side, attempting to comfort him, too, but what could be said to comfort a man whose wife was in a coma after giving birth to his son?

Garrison sniffled and said, "I have to go back."

"Will they let us see her?" a tearful Elowyn asked.

Garrison sniffled again. "I don't know, Mother. I'll…I'll see what the doctor says. You can see Junior, though. He's in the nursery. They'll let you look through the glass, but I don't know if everyone can go back at once."

"They can," a nurse said out of nowhere. "As a matter of fact, you all can come with me and I'll lead you there."

While Garrison rushed down the hallway to get back to Vivienne's side, the rest of the family followed the nurse, all of them crowding the hallway, anxious to see baby Garrison junior, while batting tears from their eyes about Vivienne's prognosis.

"Aw...look at him," Elowyn said while tears effortlessly fell from her eyes. Happy and sad ones. "He looks like all my boys did when they were babies. So beautiful." Elowyn turned to Theodore and buried her face in his chest as she cried.

"He's beautiful." Candice brought her hands to a steeple in front of her mouth.

"Looks just like Garrison," Kalina said, dabbing her eyes.

Bryson took Kalina into his embrace and held her close to him.

"I see some of Vivienne, too, especially his eyes," June observed. She sniffled.

Elowyn took a second look. "You're right, June. He does have Vivienne's eyes, doesn't he?"

With his arms crossed, Everson stood speechless next to his father.

Barringer stood the closest to the observation window, staring at his new, little nephew. For a split second, he imagined he was looking at his own son. Then his thoughts quickly went back to Vivienne and Garrison. Now he knew why Garrison was leaving the company. And he also realized he'd been selfish, trying to make Garrison feel guilty for doing so. Garrison was dealing with the possibility of losing his wife, a very real possibility, and all Barringer could think about, at the time, was the company.

Barringer walked away from his family and headed down the hallway alone. As he retreated back through the maternity waiting room, he saw Calista sitting down, her face hidden by her hands, weeping. Everything in him wanted to run to her, pull her into his arms and convince her that he would be a better man. That, if she came back to him, things would be different. He shook off the feeling. He knew in his arms was the last place she wanted to be and perhaps not even last. She didn't want him to console her. He couldn't be a husband to her when he had her. When she needed him. Why did he have a sudden urge to be one now?

Reluctantly, he walked right pass her, out of the waiting room and to the elevator he took down to the main floor, quickly exiting the hospital. Air, that's what he needed – a lot of air. As he walked towards his car, he pulled in all the air he wanted until he sat in his car and punched the steering wheel. Tonight, Calista made it apparent that she had no desire to come home. Not only was he certain he'd lost his wife. He was on the verge of losing his sister-in-law.

Chapter 14

With a broken voice and eyes swimming with tears, Garrison stood in front of family and friends who came to pay their last respects to Vivienne. "On behalf of our family, I want to thank you all for coming here to honor the life of my sweet Vivienne." His voice faded. "Sorry. This is perhaps the hardest thing I've ever had to do in my life."

Garrison took a moment to get himself together before he said, "Vivienne was my best friend. My beautiful wife. My lover. My everything. She was brilliant. Loved to sing. Travel with me. She used to talk about us retiring on an island somewhere, living out our final days in paradise. She loved life. Lived it to the fullest. When I first met her, she was fishing." He smirked. "That's right. Everyone who knew Vivienne knew she loved fishing, as do I. So one day, I'm at the dock and I see her, alone with one of those big straw hats and a pair of sunglasses. I first noticed her because her fishing pole was better than mine and I remember thinking, who is this woman with a better fishing pole than mine?"

He smiled while tears ran down his face. He wiped them away and continued, "Instead of fishing that day, I watched her fish. I was intrigued. She was reeling them in, had caught five impressive trout. She must've felt me looking at her because she turned around and said: *You're not going to try today?* The way she said it made me realize that that particular day wasn't the first time she saw me out there fishing, so I responded: *Not today. Besides, I think you've caught everything. What time is dinner?*"

Garrison smiled, remembering. "The smile that came to her face was the most beautiful smile I'd ever seen on a woman and I knew then that even though I didn't know her name, even though all I knew about this woman was that she liked to fish, I knew she would be my wife. Now she's—"

Garrison cleared his throat, looked at his son cradled in his mother's arms and said, "I was going to say she's gone, but then I look out at my mother and see my son in her arms. My wife isn't gone because she left me a gift – this beautiful baby boy. Vivienne was the embodiment of love and she loved me with a fervor that can never be matched. So today, instead of mourning, let's learn from Vivienne's example of love, for she loved a son in which she never got to meet. John 15:13 states there's no greater love than to lay down one's life for his friends. Vivienne did that for her son. For our son. We should take a lesson from her and love each other that much – so much we would be willing to die for each other. Life is short. Short in the aspect of years and short in the sense that we never know when it will end. One day we're here, the next day we're the product of memories. So let's love each other because tomorrow isn't promised to any of us. The last thing you want to do is live with regrets." Garrison looked at Barringer when he said those last few statements. He pinched the corner of his eyes and walked away from the podium.

* * *

Later in the evening, close family and friends gathered at Garrison's home and over a meal, they talked about the good times they'd shared with Vivienne. After a few hours, people were leaving – friends of the family, that is. The family remained.

Candice held Junior in her arms.

Elowyn sat next to her, eyes still weary.

June watched Everson exit the front door with his cell phone to his ear. She wondered what was so urgent.

Calista sat next to Kalina, talking about random things. Anything to avoid the sadness of the situation and to keep from looking up at Barringer again. He had been staring at her for the last thirty minutes, like he was reading her lips. A blanket of warmth consumed her as she pretended his gaze had no effect on her.

"He's going to need us in the coming weeks. Months, even," Bryson said as he walked up to Barringer. He was speaking about Garrison, but he wasn't sure if Barringer was aware of that. Barringer was zoned out, eyes fixated on Calista. Every now and then, he'd catch her gaze and she would simply look away.

"It would probably be more beneficial if you actually talked to her instead of stared," Bryson told him.

"She doesn't want to talk. She got this independent air about herself now like she doesn't need me," Barringer said, watching Calista get up and head for the kitchen.

"She needs you. You...you can't let your pride get in the way when you love someone, Barry." He was speaking from experience. When he'd fallen in love with Kalina, she rejected him, but he didn't let that stop him from pursuing her and now, they were happily married. His brother could have a happy marriage if his ego wasn't so big.

* * *

Calista stepped out onto the porch where she saw Garrison sitting on the steps, staring out into the backyard. She hadn't had an opportunity to talk to him since Vivienne's passing and although she didn't want to bring up anything she and Vivienne talked about that day at the restaurant, she knew she had to at some point.

She took a step down, sat next to him and said, "You gave a good eulogy, Gary."

Garrison turned to look at the woman who would be the fill-in mother to his son – his ex-girlfriend and sister-in-law, Calista. "Thanks, Cali."

"You're welcome."

After a few minutes of silence, Garrison said, "I'm going to need your help."

"I know. I promised Vivienne I would be there for Junior."

Garrison nodded. "We'll meet one day next week and talk about it."

"Okay. Until then, I want you to know if you need anything you can call me, okay?"

Garrison nodded again.

Calista took his right hand in her left. "I mean it, Gary."

He turned to look at her, connecting their vision.

"If you need anything, I don't care if it's just to talk, you can call me."

A small smile appeared on his face. "I appreciate that."

"Okay." She released his hand and continued down the steps, preferring to walk around the house to get to her car instead of going back inside and seeing Barringer again. He stared at her enough for one night.

Chapter 15

Three Months Later

"Hey, Gary," Calista said, standing at the door, gently bouncing a sleeping baby Garrison, Junior in her arms. Garrison had arrived to pick up his son. "Just a sec. Let me get his things."

He'd usually stand outside the door like he was afraid to come in for some reason – like it was politically incorrect to be inside of her apartment alone with her, but today, the first time in three months, he stepped in and closed the door.

The move surprised Calista. "The diaper bag is right there on the couch. He just had his bottle and has been sound asleep for...umm...about twenty minutes now."

"Okay," Garrison said, sitting down.

"Oh. You're staying?"

"I have nowhere to be," he said.

"Okay," Calista said. *Guess there's no use in putting Junior in his car seat.* He smiled. She would get to hold him a little while longer. It didn't take long for her to grow attached to Junior. After the first few days of keeping him, she was hooked. His baby smell, those cooing noises, his little hands and feet – she loved him already.

"How was he today?" Garrison asked.

"A piece of cake. He does get fussy when he's hungry. I imagine he gets that from his daddy."

Garrison grinned.

"Speaking of food, have you eaten? I made some barbecue chicken and mashed potatoes. I can warm some for you."

"That would be great. I haven't had a home-cooked meal in...can't tell you when."

Calista walked over to Garrison and said, "Here. Hold your little man." She was careful while transitioning the baby from her arms to his.

Garrison carefully cradled Junior's head into the palm of his hand and while holding him, he bent forward to kiss his cheek. Then he lowered Junior to the car seat before standing, looking around the apartment. He never did that before either – never paid much attention to how small her apartment was in relation to where she'd moved from. Barringer had the biggest house of them all.

Calista set the microwave to two minutes, then turned around to see Garrison eyeing up her apartment. "I know it isn't much, but it'll due. It's only me."

Garrison nodded. "It's plenty for one person."

"And a part-time baby."

Garrison grinned. "Right. And a part-time baby."

The microwave dinged. Calista removed his plate of hot chicken and mashed potatoes and set it on the table – the two-chair dinette in the kitchen. The area wasn't big enough to fit a four-chair table set.

Garrison sat down, looked at the food and said, "Mmm, this smells delicious."

"It used to be one of Barringer's favorites," Calista said.

"Speaking of Barringer, when was the last time you two talked?" Garrison took a bite of the chicken, mumbled how good it was and licked his fingers. He looked up at her, waiting for an answer to his question.

"Um…"

"That long, huh?"

Calista nodded. "Last time we talked, we were in the waiting room at the hospital when…when—"

"When Vivienne was in labor," Garrison finished saying for her when he realized she was hesitant to do so.

"Yes, so three months."

"Yeah. Three months," Garrison said, staring blankly at her for a moment. He returned his attention to the food.

"Can I get you something to drink?" Calista asked.

"A glass of water will be fine."

"Okay," she said standing. She took a Styrofoam cup from the cabinet and filled it with ice and water before placing it on the table next to his plate.

"Thank you, Cali."

"You're welcome. Sorry I don't have glasses. I don't see a point in buying any when these cups work just fine."

"It's okay. I'm not picky."

She smiled while watching him drink then decided to ask, "So how have you been coping?"

Garrison shrugged. "How are you coping being without Barry?"

"It's not the same, Gary. My situation is much more different than yours."

"I wasn't trying to imply it was the same. I was simply asking a question."

"Why?"

"Because you and my brother have been married for half a decade and now, you're here and have completely started over from scratch. So, how are you coping?"

Calista expelled a breath. She didn't know she'd be talking about the life and times and Calista and Barringer with Garrison, but maybe it was his way of avoiding any and everything that involved Vivienne. Seemed that's all everyone wanted to talk about whenever he came around and it must've been a pain to do so. So she decided to answer him as truthfully as she could. "Honestly, I could be better. It's not like I wanted to leave Barringer. I still love him. I told him I did, but I'm too valuable to be third place to a man."

"Ouch. If you're third, who's first and second?"

"Well, first is his job, second is his money and all the material things he buys with it." Calista watched as Garrison finished the last piece of chicken she'd given him. "I have more if you would like."

"You have more?"

"Yeah. I cooked a big pan of it."

"Why, when it's just you here?"

"Force of habit. Barringer always had a big appetite, so I'm used to cooking extra whenever I do cook. You want more?"

"Yeah. I'll take more."

Calista stood up, removed the pan of chicken from the fridge and the Tupperware container of mashed potatoes, took his plate, refilled it and warmed it in the microwave again. While his food heated up, she quickly stepped over to the living room to check on Junior. As she walked back to the kitchen, the microwave dinged. She retrieved the food and set the plate on the table in front of Garrison.

She took the chair opposite of him again, watching him eat.

"I quit," he said, steadily chewing.

"What?"

"My job at Blackstone Financial. I resigned. Barringer wasn't happy about it, but I did what I had to do."

Calista nodded. "If you resigned, what do you do after you drop off Junior with me?"

"Run errands. Sleep. Mostly sleep. I don't have a lot of motivation to do anything these days."

"Whatever happened to your dream of owning your own consulting business?"

A smile came to his face. "You still remember that?" he asked curiously.

"Of course I remember. We did date for almost two years, Gary. I remember a lot about you."

Garrison stared at her and she held his gaze, waiting for him to say something, but he didn't. Just stared.

Finally, she looked away, feeling her cheeks redden in the process. *Crap, what was that?*

"Like what?"

"Huh?" she asked, glancing up at him again.

"What do you remember about me?"

"Uh...nothing," Calista said, standing. "I think I heard my phone. I'll be right back." She grabbed her phone from the coffee table then rushed to get into her bedroom, closing the door. She palm-slapped herself in the forehead and sat on the bed. Why had she brought up anything pertaining to their past? "Not a smart move, Calista," she whispered.

After she shook it off, she left her phone on the nightstand before joining him in the kitchen. Before she could get a word out, he said, "I'm sorry if I made you feel uncomfortable. Wasn't my intent."

"No, it's fine," Calista said sitting down at the table again though she was a bit uncomfortable. She had a past with Garrison. And, by looks only, he reminded her so much of her husband – of Barringer. Dark. Chocolate.

Alluring. Physically fit. The difference between the brothers was, while Garrison was more mild-tempered, Barringer was brash, argumentative and somewhat of a perfectionist. If they could swap personalities, Barringer would make the perfect husband. But what was she really saying?

Stop it, Calista. What are you thinking?

As Garrison neared his final bites, relief settled her stomach. He'd be leaving soon. She could handle a few more minutes of small talk. "Junior is a good sleeper."

"He is," Garrison said in agreement. "Once he's fed, burped and changed, he'll kill some sleep."

"That's true." Calista watched Garrison wipe his mouth with a paper towel.

"That was delicious," he said. "Whenever you decide to cook, remember me, girl."

Calista laughed. "Okay. I will." She held his vision again. "So how have you been doing, you know, with everything?"

Garrison glared lightly and said, "It's okay to say Vivienne's name, Cali."

"Oh. Okay. I didn't know if I should, or how you felt about it and—" Calista blew a breath. "Sorry for making this awkward."

"Forgiven. Let's see...ah...some days I'm good. Some days I really miss her. She was a part of me, and she left me with a beautiful son."

Calista nodded.

"The weeks immediately following the funeral were the hardest. For the first month, I cried...not ashamed to admit that."

"You shouldn't be ashamed. It's good to cry. I know men like to play the macho role, but crying is good. Emotion is good." She could only wish Barringer showed his true emotions. He was more like a cold, corporate robot than a loving husband. Hence, their separation.

"I can't thank you enough for quitting your new job to take care of Junior on a full-time basis. I know it was a tough decision to make."

Calista shrugged. "I was only there for a month."

"Well, I hope the money Vivienne and I set aside for his care is enough for you to live off of and take care of Junior at the same time."

"It's more than enough. In fact, I think it's too much. I would've made due without it."

"Nonsense."

"Seriously, Gary. I made Vivienne a promise, and it's one I intend on keeping."

Garrison finished drinking his water.

"Was it your idea for me to take care of the baby?" Calista inquired.

Garrison shook his head. "It was Vivienne's idea, but I agreed to it. She knew how much you wanted to be a mother, so it made sense. I'm glad she chose you. You have a way with children."

"Thanks." Calista glanced at the clock. The time was close to eleven. Garrison looked too relaxed to leave. He leaned back in the chair while stretching his arms above his head, yawning.

She smiled. "You got the *itis* now?"

He laughed, lowering his arms. "Yeah. I got it. A good meal will do that to a man. You mind if I crashed on the couch tonight?"

"Uh...um..." *Wait, is he serious, or is this a part of the joke?*

"I'll stay out of your way," Garrison added. "You have extra clothes and formula here for Junior, right?"

Oh goodness. He is serious. Calista swallowed. "Ye-yeah."

"Then would it be okay?" he asked again.

"Yeah. That's fine. I don't have extra blankets or anything."

"I don't need any. I just don't want to be *there* tonight. Alone, again. I want to...I need to talk. To you."

"To me?" she asked, eyebrows raised.

"Yes."

"Gary, you have your brothers. Kalina told me Bryson has been trying to get ahold of you. And Everson. Candice. Your parents. You have plenty of people to talk to."

"I do, but I want to talk to you. The night of the repast, you held my hand and told me if ever I needed to talk I could come to you, right?"

Calista smiled warmly. "Right." It took him three months, but he finally wanted to talk.

Garrison stood up and walked over to the living room where he checked on Junior, adjusting him slightly in the car seat before he sat on the sandy brown, microfiber couch.

Calista followed him, choosing to sit on the loveseat. She looked over at him. His long, outstretched legs nearly touched her coffee table. He threw his head back and spread his arms out on the backrest of the couch. "So, what do you want to talk about?"

"The fact that I have yet to visit her grave, and I don't know if I should. If I do, what do I say?"

"Well—"

"And what am I supposed to tell my son when he's older? When he asks, *where's mommy*? What am I supposed to say?"

"That's years down the road, Gary."

"I know, but this is what I think about. It's constantly on my mind." Garrison released a frustrated breath.

"When he's old enough to understand, you tell him the truth. He'll learn the truth anyway, so there's no use in keeping it from him. And it's a personal choice whether you want to visit her grave, but I wouldn't be opposed to going with you for support."

"You would?"

"Yes, and I'm sure any one of the family would. I loved Vivienne, too. Loved her like a sister. We all loved her. Still do."

A half smile touched his lips.

"And you can visit her grave whenever you want, however many times you want."

Garrison scrubbed his hands down his face. "I'm going to let you get to bed. I'm overstaying my welcome. I'm aware of that."

"No, it's fine," Calista said standing. And it was fine. She was uneasy at first, but the truth of the matter was, Garrison needed her and she wanted to be there for him. "I hope you have a good night's sleep."

"Thanks again, Calista."

"You're welcome, Gary." Calista turned around to head for her bedroom when she had a thought. "Gary."

"Yes?" he said. He'd already stretched out on the couch, his body expanding the length of it. "Have you thought about going back to work?"

"At Blackstone Financial?"

"Yes," she nodded.

He sat up a little. "No. Why?"

"Because working can help keep your mind off of...things."

"You mean Vivienne."

Calista nodded. "Yes. Vivienne. It helps to know you're working to accomplish something...that you're making a difference and from what I've heard, Barry could use the help."

Garrison lowered his head again, staring up at the ceiling. "I haven't given much thought to going back."

"Well, think about it," she said. "Oh, and I'll take Junior in my room so you can get a full night's sleep."

"You don't have to do that, Cali. You've already watched him the entire day."

"It's okay. I don't mind it. I've been waiting a long time to take care of a baby. Looks like this is as close as I'm going to get." She bent forward and scooped Junior out of his car seat, carefully securing his head and neck, cradling him in her arms. "Plus, his crib is in my room…can't have my baby cramped up in a car seat all night."

My baby…

"Well, if you insist." Exhausted and full, Garrison closed his eyes.

Calista continued on to her bedroom whispering, "That's right, little Gary…come on to Auntie Cali's room so daddy can get some sleep."

Chapter 16

Alcohol, music and sports – the combination of the three should've been enough to level Barringer out for an hour or so. At least that's what Bryson thought since he'd chosen to meet Barringer at Bayside Billiards to talk. He wanted to get an idea of how his brother was holding up with the company and with his marriage.

Barringer took a sip of Southern Comfort. "How's business at the tree service?"

"It's going pretty good," Bryson said. "Staying busy. No complaints. What about you? How's life at Blackstone Financial Services?"

"Hold on," Barringer said while he keyed a reply to a text from Colton. Colton had called him when he couldn't reach Calista. Before their separation, Calista had scheduled Colton and his painting crew to come by the house (now Barringer's house), to paint two bedrooms. After texting Calista's address to

Colton and instructing him to go there to talk to her about the upcoming paint job, Colton responded back with a single question mark.

Barringer placed his phone down next to his glass, returning his attention to Bryson. "What were you saying?"

"I was asking how business was going at Blackstone Financial."

"Oh." Barringer shook his head and took another sip of his drink. "It's not going good. For the first time in the company's history, we may need to lay off some workers."

"How many?"

"Don't know yet. If I had to guess, I'd say between fifty and a hundred."

"Man...that many?"

"Yep. If Candice hadn't worked so hard to secure the Telmark deal, it would probably be more than that." Barringer picked up his phone, deciding to reply to Colton's question mark.

Barringer: Long story. Tell you about it later.

"Have you reached out to anyone at Blakeney?" Bryson asked.

"I have. They told me they're getting a better deal with advanced technology and if we couldn't top it, there was no need to discuss anything further." Barringer looked at his phone.

Colton: Maybe I shouldn't be discussing

anything about the house with Cali since she no longer lives there. Makes no sense.

Barringer frowned, shook his head and responded back:

Barringer: Just go.

He placed his phone down again.

"Who did they end up going with, anyway?" Bryson inquired.

"What?"

"Blakeney," Bryson said. "Who did they sign with?"

"TCC out of Asheville, North Carolina."

Bryson's brows rose. "TCC as in The Champion Corporation?"

Did Barringer even hear his question? He was looking at his phone. Again.

Bryson glanced at Barringer's cell phone then back at him.

"Colton's texting me," Barringer said, grunting about how much he hated texting. "He wants to know about the paint job Calista scheduled for some of the bedrooms. I told him to go by her place, but you know how Colton is. I'm surprised he hasn't called me yet."

Just then, his phone rang.

"Looks like you talked him up," Bryson said.

Barringer let out a rough sigh. "Colton, just go over there and talk to her, man," he answered.

"You don't have her number?" Colton

inquired.

"No, I don't."

"In that case, I'm canceling the job."

"Colt, don't cancel the job."

"I booked four hours for this slot, Barry. If you don't need the rooms painted—"

"Go by her place in the morning, man," Barringer interrupted him to say.

"Why?" Colton snapped. "To get her to make design decisions on your house, because it is *your* house now. Why would Calista care what color your walls are? She can't even stand the sight of you? You really think she gives a crap about your walls?"

Colton's words left Barringer speechless as he thought about what his rude, straightforward cousin was telling him. Calista had been gone for three months. She showed no indications of coming back. She didn't call or text him. While he didn't have Calista's number, she still had his, and she made it apparent that she didn't intend on using it.

"Look, I'll go over there in the morning and see what she has to say. Jeez..." Colton said before he hung up.

Barringer mumbled his frustration and placed the phone on the bar next to his glass. "What were you saying?" he asked Bryson.

"You said Blakeney went with TCC. I was asking you if that was—"

"The Champion Corporation. Yes, that's correct. You're familiar with them?"

Bryson nodded. "Some of my guys did some landscaping at the resort TCC owns on Carolina

Beach...had no idea they were in the finance market."

"According to their website, they're into everything," Barringer said. He'd researched the company, finding out that Dante Champion was the CEO and President. His brother, Dimitrius Champion was in charge of accounts and then there was Desmond Champion who headed up marketing.

"Maybe a meeting with them would give you some insight into what their aim is."

"Their aim is what every company's *aim* is...to make money. I can't have a meeting with the competition."

"You can if you have something viable to offer."

"Something viable like what? Should I just hand them all of our clients, Bryce?"

"That's not what I'm saying, man."

Barringer tossed back his drink, finishing it.

"I still can't believe Vivienne's gone," Bryson said.

"Me either. By the way, have you heard from Garrison? I tried to call him the other day. Got voicemail."

"You should probably go to his house. I stopped by there yesterday...talked with him for a minute. He's still trying to get himself in order. Said he wanted to get Vivienne's clothes and things together soon...donate them to charity or something. You know Cali's been watching the baby."

Barringer nodded. "Yeah. Guess she finally gets a baby after all, huh? Too bad I couldn't give her one."

"Don't look at it like that, man. When was the last time you talked to Calista?"

"At the hospital when Vivienne was in labor. Saw her at the funeral and afterwards at Gary's house, but didn't say anything to her."

"Why not?"

He shrugged. "She was pretty clear about us when we last spoke. She doesn't even wear her wedding rings anymore."

"Yeah, man, but did you tell her about the baby situation?"

"Why? She already left me. What's the point?"

"Are you *that* prideful? Come on, Barry. Tell her, man. Don't you want her back?"

"No woman has ever left me," he touted.

"Do you want her back or not?"

Barringer spun his empty glass on the wooden bar top. "Yes. I want her back."

"Then get her back, man. You can't put all this time and separation between the two of you and expect things to fall into place."

"You must be mistaken. I didn't leave her. She left me. She put the separation between us. And she changed her number so I couldn't contact her. I can't even pick up the phone and call my wife."

Bryson shrugged. "So what? You know where she's living now, right?"

Barringer sighed heavily. "Right."

"Then looks like you need to pay Calista a visit." Bryson took out his wallet and placed a twenty-dollar bill on the bar for their drinks.

He stood up, patting Barringer on the shoulder. "Come on. Let's get out of here."

"What's the rush?" Barringer asked, not wanting to go home to an empty house just yet.

"I have a wife waiting for me at home, man. And you have to go home and figure out a way to get yours back."

"Easier said than done."

"It is, but you have to try."

Barringer stood up, walking with Bryson towards the exit.

Chapter 17

In the morning, Calista tied a robe over the blue cotton pajama set she'd worn to bed. She took a diaper and a package of wipes from Junior's diaper bag. Looking down at him, she smiled. He smiled back, showing her those big bright eyes and pink gums.

"I see you smiling at me beautiful baby boy," she said, lifting him from the crib and lowering him gently to the bed. "You have eyes like you mommy. You know that?"

She proceeded to take off his messy diaper and clean him up with baby wipes before sliding the new diaper underneath him, fastening it. "Now we have to find you some clothes, little man."

She took a blue onesie from the diaper bag and maneuvered his little hands and feet into it until she could clasp the buttons. "There. Now you're all clean and comfy. Let's see if daddy's awake. Do you think daddy's awake?"

When Calista opened the door, Garrison was sitting upright on the couch, checking his cell phone.

Garrison looked up when he heard the door open and said, "Yeah. Daddy's awake." He smiled.

Calista smiled back. "These thin apartment walls…"

"Yeah, that's apartment living. I especially enjoyed listening to you sing to him last night. I think you put *me* to sleep after Twinkle, Twinkle Little Star." Garrison grinned.

Calista did too, with a red, embarrassed face. "Sorry. I don't have the best singing voice."

"Are you kidding me? You sounded beautiful. Like a loving mother."

"Thanks, Gary. Did you sleep okay on the couch?"

"Yeah. It did the trick. It's comfortable."

"Good. I'm glad. Um, do you want coffee or anything?"

"No. I should actually get going," Garrison said, standing tall walking up to her to take Junior out of her arms.

"You're taking him?" Calista said, feeling like he was losing a piece of herself.

"Yeah. Figured I'd give you the day off since you did day and night duty. We'll have a father-son day today, right Junior?"

"Okay. Let me get his car seat."

Once Garrison secured his son in the seat, Calista handed him the pacifier and said, "You don't want to leave without this. It's his favorite."

"Thanks."

She walked to the front door, opened it for him, but he set the car seat down for a moment to hug her, and it wasn't one of those carefree hugs. He really embraced her, squeezing her snugly in between his arms while he palmed the back of her head, pulling her against his chest.

Calista squeezed him back.

Before they separated, Garrison left a kiss at her temple, then looked into her eyes. "Thank you."

Calista knew his 'thank you' actually meant something, because she didn't have to do what she was doing. She could've declined the responsibility of taking care of Junior. Kept her job. Her freedom. But she hadn't. She went above and beyond for Junior and for him. "You're welcome, Gary."

He smiled.

She swallowed the lump in her throat when she saw him glance at her lips. Her breath quickened when he leaned down, but relief rushed through her when she realized he was leaning down to pick up the car seat. He wasn't trying to kiss her.

"See you later, Cali."

"Yep. Later," she told him.

After watching him walk away, Calista closed the door, closed her eyes and covered her face with her hands. Now she could breathe.

* * *

After watching Garrison drive away, Colton decided to get out of his work van. He'd been watching the exchange between Calista and Garrison, confused about why Garrison was leaving Calista's apartment at six in the morning, hugging her tight like they didn't want to turn each other loose.

Ringing the doorbell, he waited a moment then saw Calista snatch the door open and say, "Did you forget—? Oh," she said with bright, surprised eyes when she realized it wasn't Garrison. Colton was standing at her door. "Colton? What are you doing here?"

"Your husband sent me here to ask you about the color schemes for the bedrooms. I would've called you but—"

"You don't have my new number," she finished saying. "Right. Sorry about that."

"So did you still want to—?"

"You'll have to discuss that with Barringer. I don't live there anymore and I have no clue why he sent you here to discuss anything with me."

Colton scratched his head. "Y'all are really screwing with my schedule."

"Sorry, Colton. I should've called and cancelled, but it completely slipped my mind with the funeral and everything...can you come in for a sec?"

He frowned. "Why?"

"Because I want to write you a check for the missed appointment. I know how valuable your time is. Come in."

His expression softened as he stepped

inside. He looked around, scoped out the place. When Calista opened her bedroom door to get her purse, Colton saw the unmade bed. He didn't want to jump to conclusions, but it nagged him to have seen Garrison leaving so early in the morning and now an unmade bed? Then Calista had on a robe – what was going on?

"Here you go," she said, handing Colton a check.

Colton took it from her grasp. He looked at it. Eight-hundred, seventy-five dollars.

"I know your cancellation fee is a few hundred lower, but I owe you."

"Thanks," he said, sliding the check inside his back pocket. "Hey, did I see Garrison leave a few minutes ago?"

"Yeah. He was picking up Junior," she decided to tell him. It sounded a lot better than: *He spent the night. With me and the baby. In my one-bedroom apartment.*

"Oh, okay," Colton said, though he thought it was strange that Garrison would be there so early to pick up the baby. "So you and Barringer..."

"What about me and Barringer?"

"Are you officially over?" Colton inquired.

Calista grimaced. "Nothing's official. We're just taking a break."

"You mean, *you're* taking a break."

"If you want to put it that way, yes. I guess so."

"A three-month break..."

Calista narrowed her eyes. "Where are you

going with this, Colton?"

"I'm not around you guys much and I don't know you all that well, Calista, but I do know Barringer. I was at the wedding. I know how much he loves you. The man told me he would never get married. Then you came along. He couldn't resist you. Still can't. If you took the time to talk to him, you'll see the hurt in his eyes, hear the pain in his voice. He's my cousin, yes. He's irritating, hard to get along with at times, but I love him like a brother. Give him a chance. He still loves you. Why else do you think he wanted me to come here and talk to you about painting those bedrooms?"

Just to irritate me, Calista thought.

"You're both prideful," Colton said.

"I'm not prideful. I'm hurt."

"Well, so is he. Get over it."

"Excuse me?"

"You heard me. If you didn't want to *hurt* so much, maybe you shouldn't have gotten married."

"What is that supposed to mean?" Calista said, not following him.

"Married people are supposed to experience tribulation, right? Read that a long time ago in the Bible, perhaps the reason I'm still single." Or maybe the reason he was still single was because his ex-girlfriend, Miriam, left him to be with a man who, according to her, had more ambition than settling to be a small town painter. Colton removed the check from his pocket, looked at it and said, "Tell you what...I'll keep this check to use as payment on the job when you and Barry are ready to complete the rooms."

"You don't have to do that, Colton."

"I know I don't. Anyway, I have to get back to work. I'll see you later, Calista." He turned to head for the door.

"Okay. Later, Colton." She rubbed her eyes listening to her phone ring from the bedroom. She swiftly walked there, answering when she saw it was Kalina. After exchanging greetings, she told Kalina about her conversation with Colton. Kalina couldn't believe it.

"I'm serious," Calista said, setting a bowl of grits inside of the microwave. "That's what he told me."

"And we're talking about Colton?"

"Yes."

"Colton, Mean-faced Blackstone?" Kalina said.

"Yes. That Colton." Calista laughed while taking the bowl from the microwave. She sat at the kitchen table alone eating while talking to Kalina on speakerphone. "I was just as surprised as you are. Trust me."

After she'd finished laughing, Kalina said, "He's right, though. There is a passage in the Bible that points to married folk going through a lot of trials."

"Why is that? I mean, if two people love each other to the point of spending the rest of their lives together and fully committing to one another, why does so much headache come along with it?"

"Because you're both different. You have

different backgrounds, completely different outlooks on life—"

Calista rolled her eyes. "I knew I shouldn't have asked a newlywed. Bryson does anything you want him to."

"And I return the favor by doing anything he asks of me."

Calista smiled. "Aw...I remember when I used to be that way...when I was so concerned about how Barringer would feel about a particular situation before I knew how *I* felt about it. Everything was always about him, and I mean everything."

"So what happened?"

"When I realized he didn't care about how I felt, I stopped caring about how he felt. Two wrongs...blah, blah, yeah, I know, but still doesn't change the fact that I was tired of expending all of my time and energy on a man who took ev-e-ry-thing I had to give without giving me anything in return."

Calista ate more of her food, then said, "I've been thinking about Vivienne lately."

"Me too," Kalina said. "Random memories just come out of nowhere, like her and Garrison dancing together at my wedding reception. She was pregnant with Junior, and Garrison had his hands on her stomach. He loved her. He really did."

"And what's sad is, even that night, they knew about the risk...just hadn't told anyone."

"Yeah...makes you sadder to think about that." After a few moments of silence, Kalina said, "Hey, you see Garrison on a steady basis since you watch Junior all the time. How is he?"

"He seems okay on the surface, but I can tell it's eating away at him, you know. He's still mourning, and he hasn't had that moment where it actually hit him. You know what I mean?"

"You mean after the shock wears off...when the real grieving happens?"

Calista nodded.

"Yes, I know the feeling all too well. It happened to me when my mom died," Kalina said. "I just hope Garrison reaches out to someone when it happens to him because it's going to happen at some point."

"I'll try to encourage him to confide in his brothers. I'm not sure if he's been talking to any of them on a regular basis."

"Um...I don't think so. The guys have had a few game nights and, according to Bryson, Garrison never comes. Barringer is hit or miss." Kalina sighed. "I don't this feeling...like the family is falling apart. I come from a highly dysfunctional situation, so when Bryson invited me to be a part of his family, I was excited to finally have a real family. Now everything seems so strained. Vivienne is gone. Garrison is a single father now. You and Barringer split..."

"It's just a difficult time right now, Kalina. But just hold on to Bryson. Okay. He's the noblest of them all."

Kalina smiled big. "Thank you, Cali."

"And don't tell him I said that."

Kalina laughed.

"Well, now that I've finished breakfast and have been ministered to by Colton, I need to get some chores done."

"Okay, sis. I'll see you later."

"All right. Bye, girl."

Calista ended the call, then took her bowl to the sink.

Chapter 18

After finishing up laundry, most of which consisted of juniors cute, little baby clothes, Calista wound her hair in a bun and jumped in the shower. With a few errands to run, she dressed quickly, wearing a pair of printed yoga pants and a matching blue shirt. She applied gloss to her lips, grabbed her purse and opened the front door. That's when she saw him – Barringer, standing there wearing a black baseball cap so low on his head, it nearly hid his dark eyes. He was dressed casual today – had on a white shirt and a pair of dark jeans.

Goodness, he was fine. Clean-shaven. Mustache trimmed above a pair of smooth lips. Lips she remembered being succulent. Tempting and tasteful. And his dark skin beckoned her attention more so than before. Against the white shirt he wore, his skin looked extra dark, like some exotic, finger-lickin' good chocolate from the world's finest chocolatiers.

She remembered he used to joke about his complexion when they were dating, saying: *The blacker the 'Barry', the sweeter the juice.* And he wasn't lying. It had been sweet, but time and circumstances had changed him. Changed them.

Not seeing him in a while had made her appreciate his good looks, things she realized she'd taken for granted. His broad shoulders. Muscular physique that normally stayed hidden underneath expensive suits. The way he could wear a pair of jeans low on his hips. No man could wear a pair of jeans like Barringer. And no man could excite her like him. Mad and all, it didn't matter. Barringer was the only man to make her feel desire stirring in her belly.

"Barry, what are you doing here?" she asked finally after a full minute, the longest minute in the history of time, had passed between them.

Barringer stood there, staring at Calista, not saying anything for a moment, just loving the way her shirt matched her light skin tone and how those pants showed off her curves. He stared into her eyes, caught under her spell. Who couldn't she captivate with her beauty? With those alluring, pink, sugary lips of hers and big, black eyes, smooth as silk skin and luscious, dark black hair tinted with a hint of burgundy?

"Barry?"

"Did I catch you at a bad time?" he asked when he saw her purse on her shoulder.

The sound of his voice made her tingle all over, but she couldn't let him see what kind of effect he was having on her. She was still mad at him. "Actually, I was on my way out to run some errands. Why?"

He took a step forward. "You're not going to invite me in?"

I did just say I was on my way out, didn't I? She took a step back. "Sure. You can come in for a minute."

Barringer stepped inside looking around her apartment. *Nice*, he thought quietly to himself. It suited her. Decorated to her taste down to the most insignificant detail. Like the flower on the dinette in the kitchen that matched the curtains in the living room.

He took a seat on the couch and saw a baby rattle on the small, wooden coffee table. He picked it up, shook it so it did its job – rattle. He placed it back on the table. "You're still watching the baby, huh?"

Calista narrowed her eyes at him, trying to figure him out. The man didn't want children, but he was playing with a baby rattle...

"Barry, I really need to get going."

He looked up at her. "Can you sit down for a moment?"

Calista forced a breath. She dropped her bag on the floor next to the loveseat where she decided to sit.

"I know I'm intruding on your precious time," he said curtly, "But I figured since we haven't spoken in a while, *I* would make the effort. Did you talk to Colton? He called me last night to see if you still wanted those rooms painted."

"He came by this morning. I told him to talk to you about it," Calista said.

"Why did you tell him to talk to me? You usually handle those things."

"Right, but I don't live there anymore, so I don't want to overstep my boundaries. It's your house now, Barry."

"No. It's *our* home, Cali."

Calista looked at her unpainted fingernails, pondering what he'd said. *Our* home. Was he delusional? How could he think it was their home when she hadn't lived here in three months? "Okay, well I told Colton to talk to you about it since you're there. I'm not there." She looked up at him, instantly feeling herself being pulled into the depth of his eyes.

"Did you really leave me because of the baby issue?" he asked.

The baby issue. Calista frowned. She didn't want to talk about this now. She had errands to run. And why wasn't he at work? "That's part of it, yes, but there are other issues which I've already brought to your attention and I'm really not in the mood to reiterate those things to you, Barry. I have a lot to get done today and if you wanted to talk, maybe you should've—"

"Called first?" he said with raised eyebrows and contempt in his voice, "Because you changed your number, remember, so I couldn't call you."

"I changed my number because you were leaving angry voicemails and text messages."

"Why wouldn't I be angry? My wife of five years left me out of the blue, high and dry—"

Calista rolled her eyes. "High and dry…"

"Yeah. High and dry. I don't have a right to be angry?"

"You do have that right, but how does it fix anything?"

"How does living apart from me fix anything!"

Calista's face reddened in exasperation. "We're going in circles…always going in circles with senseless arguing. All I ever wanted was a family and loving husband, a real family man who valued his family…who knew how precious time was. I was twenty-nine when we married. Now, I'm thirty-five. Do you know that puts me in the high-risk category for pregnancy now? You probably don't, because you're more concerned about advancing your company to the next level to be focused on anything that concerns me." She looked up at him, catching his direct stare back at her. His eyes looked glossy. Narrowed and glossy.

Barringer folded his lips under and interlocked his fingers. "I can't have children, Calista." There, he said it. He looked her in the eyes and finally admitted it, watching a frown grow in her forehead.

"What are you talking about?" she asked, seeking clarification.

"I can't have children." When he saw her expression grow even more confused he said, "It's impossible for me to get you pregnant. I'm sterile. I shoot blanks. If you don't understand what I'm saying by now, I don't know how else to make you understand."

"B-but, every time we made love, you made sure we used birth control. You told me you weren't ready for a baby. If you knew you were sterile, why use birth control?"

Flustered, he responded, "Because I didn't want you to know. I'm sure you would've wondered why you weren't pregnant and I—"

Barringer took a breath. "I didn't want you to know I was sterile, Cali. I'd been trying different treatments for a few years and nothing worked."

"For a few years?" she asked. "Why not just tell me what was going on, Barry?"

"I couldn't."

"Why couldn't you? You made me think you didn't want children. Every time I asked about children, you told me the time wasn't right. Why not tell me the truth?"

"Because I knew you would hate me for doing so."

"I wouldn't hate you for being honest with me."

"You would," Barringer said, lowering his head. "I didn't tell you because I feared you would not have married me."

"Married you?" Calista said faintly. "You...you mean you knew about this before we got married?"

Barringer nodded shamefully. "I did."

Her expression hardened. "You knew you couldn't have children, and you didn't tell me."

"Cali—"

"Wow," she said, holding a hand over her heart. "You're such a liar, Barry."

"I knew you wouldn't want me if you found out. So I decided not to tell you and, instead, proceeded with the treatment so I could give you a family. I wanted a family, too."

Calista's eyes flooded with tears. "So you were dishonest with me right from the start."

"Cali, I'm sorry."

Calista squeezed tears from her eyes. The sight of her doing so ripped Barringer's heart into two.

"Say something."

Calista sniffled. "There's nothing to say, at least nothing that'll be beneficial at the moment. Just—" She sniffled. "Just go, Barry."

"Calista, I—"

"Please leave," she said softly. Sniffling.

Barringer stood up. "For whatever it's worth, I'm sorry. I didn't mean to deceive you." He stared at her for a long moment, watching her cry. When she covered her face with her hands and whimpered, he turned around and headed for the door.

Chapter 19

When Calista was able to clear her eyes and hide the puffiness and redness that had settled underneath with concealer and powder foundation, she proceeded out of the door. She was in a daze while shopping for groceries, pushing the cart up and down lanes, thinking about what Barringer told her – that he couldn't have children.

She took two boxes of lasagna noodles from the shelf, dropped them into her cart.

I can't have children. I'm sterile...

She couldn't get those words out of her head. If a person couldn't have a child and knew a potential marriage partner wanted a child, wasn't that person under obligation to be straightforward, upfront and honest?

Not Barringer.

He held the secret for years. Said he took measures to reverse his infertility, but the treatments hadn't worked.

I didn't tell you because I feared you would not have married me...

She couldn't say what she would've done at the time. Too bad he didn't give her a chance to make that decision. Calista blew a breath, attempting to force away sadness. "Okay, Calista. Keep it together. You can't be crying in this store."

She waved her hands in front of her face to help dry the tears forming in her eyes. And then she remembered to head back over to the wine aisle to grab a bottle of Sangria.

* * *

Back at her apartment, she unpacked groceries then sat down on the couch where Barringer had sat. Tingles ran through her again. She could still smell his scent. Gosh, she missed his scent. It didn't matter know angry she was at him. How much he annoyed her. She didn't even care that he'd lied. She missed him, and had he told her about his *condition* before they married, they could've dealt with it together. Instead, he chose to do it all on his own, just like he'd made the decision to take over his father's company without even consulting her.

She looked at her purse when she heard her phone ringing from it. Instead of getting up to get it, she closed her eyes and bathed in Barringer's scent, trying to guess who could be calling.

It wasn't Barringer. She still hadn't given

him her number. Maybe it was Kalina. Or what about June? She hadn't spoken with her in a couple days.

"Nah, it's not June," Calista decided. "I bet, it's Candice. That's who it is. Candice."

She pulled herself up and fumbled around in her bag until she found her phone. It had since stopped ringing, so she looked through the call log and saw she had been wrong about the caller. It was Garrison.

A smile came to her face when she thought about Junior. While she was able to get a lot of work done today, she still missed him. In some ways, she felt like Junior was her child. She loved him. Took care of him any time Garrison needed her to. It was the least she could do.

Quickly dialing him back, Garrison answered, "Hey, thought you were coming by this evening?"

"You did?" Calista said, standing upright, her heart beating fast. "I'm sorry. Do you need to be somewhere?"

"No, but I thought I told you about helping me with Vivienne's clothes."

"Oh, ah...I don't recall you telling me that, but if you're going to be there, I can come over," she said, rotating her arm to look at her watch.

"I don't plan on going anywhere."

"Okay. Give me about thirty minutes."

"Okay, Cali."

"How's my chubby cheeks?"

Garrison grinned. "He's sleeping, but he should be good and ready to eat, probably by the time you get here if you want to cure your baby itch."

"Good," Calista said excited. It didn't matter she was in a funky mood because of Barringer's admission. She would get to see her baby today.

Her baby.

"I'll see you soon," Garrison said.

"Yep. Bye."

Calista hung up the phone, smiling from ear to ear. She wasted no time retouching her makeup. Her eyes were still puffy from the bomb Barringer dropped on her earlier. Nose still red. She couldn't leave the house like that. So, after making sure she looked decent, she took her purse from the loveseat and stepped into a pair of shoes she'd left by the front door before heading to her car.

Chapter 20

"Hey, Barry," Bryson said, opening the door to let his brother in.

Without saying a word, Barringer proceeded towards Bryson's man cave.

"This is a surprise," Bryson said, following him. "What's going on?"

"I told her," Barringer said, falling lazily into a leather recliner. "I told Calista I couldn't have children."

"When?" Bryson asked, taking two beers from a black mini-fridge, handing Barringer one of them. He sat in the recliner next to him and popped the top off of his beer.

"Earlier." Barringer opened his beer, took a long swig from it. "You should've seen the look on her face. I can't get that image out of my head. It's like I could see her heart breaking right in front of me. She was hurt, disappointed—"

Bryson looked at his brother for a moment.

He didn't know how to help him out of this. "Did she say anything?"

"Yeah. She asked me why I didn't tell her before we married. I think that hurt her the most." Barringer slowly shook his head. "All of this is just too much to deal with, man. My wife leaves me. I lose the company's biggest client. Gary quit."

Bryson sat straight up. "Gary quit?"

"Well, he said he wasn't coming back. So, yeah. He quit. Said he needed to focus on Junior."

"Well, don't worry about that too much. Garrison is a worker. He's not the type to sit around and twiddle his thumbs. Just give him some time. He lost his wife. He needs time."

"I lost my wife, too," Barringer said. "I don't get to take time off."

"Two completely different situations, Barry. Vivienne died. Have you even sat down and spoken with Gary since the funeral?"

"Haven't had time."

Bryson raised a brow. "Haven't had time? Come on, Barringer. It's been like three months. You haven't had time?"

"I have a company to run."

Bryson shook his head. "Go on and finish your beer, because you're not going to like me in a few minutes."

Barringer grinned but he knew what was coming – some straight talk from his older brother. So he took a long sip of beer, then glanced over at Bryson.

"I think you need to take a step away from

BFSG. There, I said it."

"What would make you say something absurd like that?" Barringer asked.

"Easy. I don't care how much money you make...how big your house is or how many foreign cars you own, Barry. You can't replace family with money. You and Calista have built a life together, and she's been a good wife to you, man."

Barringer blew a ragged breath. "She's been gone for three months. She doesn't care about me."

"Oh, she cares about you. She loves you, but the longer she's away, the easier it becomes to *not* care. Do you feel what I'm saying right now?"

"But she doesn't want to talk—"

"You're making excuses, Barry," Bryson interrupted. "You tell yourself *she doesn't care* and *it's already over* and *she's been gone for three months* so you don't have to pour your heart out. You're stubborn like that. I know you are...know from experience. So, being on the outside looking in, I'ma tell you what I see. I see two sinking ships in your life. You're trying to save one ship, the company, while letting the other ship sink, your wife. Is BFSG more important to you than Calista?"

"I believe there's still hope for BFSG."

"And not for your marriage?" Bryson asked, looking intently at his brother.

Barringer shook his head. "You know the saying, if you love something let it go?"

"Yeah. I heard of it. Don't agree with it, but I

heard of it."

"You let Felicia go."

Bryson frowned. "Felicia left me and had no intentions on coming back. She didn't love me anymore, Barringer, and I was wise enough to know that. I'm not going to lie...it hurt. But all of that is in the past now. I got the woman I was meant to be with. Kalina is everything to me."

"I'm not Calista's *everything*. I can't give her a baby. Do you know how that makes me feel? As a man? It's like everyone is crying, poor Calista, but what about me? I want—" Barringer choked up, completely out of character for him. After taking moment to get himself together, he said, "I want to give my wife a baby. I can't do that. So I feel obligated to let her be happy with someone else."

Bryson's brows snapped together. "Are you kidding me?"

"I didn't say I *wanted* her to be with someone else. I said I feel *obligated*. I feel like I owe her that much for lying to her. Ten, twenty years from now when we don't have children and are both too old to think about having kids, I don't want to see resentment in her eyes. So, yes, I'm leaning towards letting the marriage ship sink, Bryson," Barringer swallowed hard. "BFSG still has a shot at being saved."

Bryson shook his head. "How's that?"

"I called The Champion Corporation and Desmond Champion called me back yesterday. He wants to meet with us soon."

Bryson nodded.

"You think I'm making a mistake, don't you?" Barringer asked.

"No. I think, first and foremost, you should do everything in your power to get Calista back. Second, go talk to Garrison. He may look okay on the outside, but he's hurting. And Dad...it's time you let him know what's going on with the company. It was his before he turned it over to you. It won't hurt to ask for a little advice. You don't know it all, and you can't do it all. You're overextending yourself. You're burnt out. You need a break."

"You're right. You're right." Barringer pulled in a breath and closed his eyes while slowly expelling another breath. He had a lot of decisions ahead of him, ones he wasn't sure he was ready to make.

Chapter 21

"Aw, there's my little chubby-cheeked friend," Calista said, her face aglow when she took Junior from Garrison's arms.

Garrison smiled. "I just got him out of the crib...got his bottle warming in a cup of warm water in the kitchen."

"Look at you getting the hang of this daddy thing," Calista said as she lightly bounced Junior in her arms on the way to the kitchen. Around the same time, she realized this was the first time she'd been to his house after Vivienne's funeral. She noticed he hadn't taken down wedding photos or any photos of her for that matter.

In the kitchen, Calista took Junior's bottle and tested the warmth of the milk by squirting a little on her arm. "It's perfect for you, Junior," she said, putting the nipple of the bottle close to his mouth. Junior latched on to it.

Garrison, wearing a pair of jeans and a red Polo, was standing at the entryway with his arms crossed, observing. For a moment, he thought he was seeing Vivienne there with Junior, taking care of him – feeding him and singing to him. There was no doubt in his mind that Vivienne would've been a good mother, but Calista was an excellent stand-in in her absence. "You're good with him."

Calista glanced up. "I have to be. I'm holding precious cargo," she said. "Plus, I have big shoes to fill."

Garrison smiled.

"Every time I hold Junior, I feel like Vivienne's here," she said.

"Yeah. He has her eyes." He continued on inside of the kitchen and sat on a barstool at the island. "How am I supposed to start over?" he asked, crossing his arms.

"That's a tough question, Gary."

"I know, because I ask myself that question every day and night and for the life of me, I can't answer it. I look at her pictures on the walls...all this decorating...everything you see in this house, down to the curtains were all planned and coordinated by her. How am I supposed to start over when I see these things every day? When I can't bring myself to take our wedding pictures down?"

Calista walked over and sat next to him. Adjusting Junior in her arms, she said, "It won't be easy. I mean, Vivienne was a part of us all."

"But she was *my* wife, Calista," he said in a

slightly elevated tone. "She was supposed to grow old with me. We were supposed to raise our son together."

"I know," Calista said, not knowing what else to say.

"Instead, she gives me a son, this beautiful baby boy, and she's gone." He grimaced, stood up and said, "You know where the master bedroom is. Just go in the closet and take her clothes down for me."

"Actually, I don't know where the master bedroom is," Calista said. All the times she'd visited their home and after the many family dinners Garrison and Vivienne hosted, she never wandered upstairs. There was plenty of room downstairs.

Garrison turned to look at her. He looked puzzled. Confused somehow.

"No worries, Gary. I'm sure I can find it. It's not a problem."

Garrison turned to walk away, but stopped abruptly, looked at her once more without her knowledge, while she bounced his son in her arms. Then he continued on outside.

* * *

After she had finished feeding Junior, she made sure to burp him before taking him to his room. She remembered how proud Vivienne was after completing his room, but this was the first time she'd seen it. She loved how alphabet blocks spelled out his name on the wall above the crib. The baseball curtains, blue walls, the area rug that was designed like a baseball – it all looked like something Vivienne would do.

Calista took a few steps down the hallway into what looked like the master bedroom. There wasn't a thing out of place in the immaculate room. Nothing. The bed was made. The cream carpet didn't have a stain on it. Even the perfume, makeup and other items on her vanity were properly placed. She doubted Garrison was sleeping in there. He probably couldn't bring himself to do so.

She stepped into the massive, walk-in closet. Garrison's clothes were to the left. Vivienne's to the right. There were at least twenty pairs of shoes, mostly heels. And then she saw jackets, sweaters, jeans and purses. Centered in the closet was a long, ivory-colored leather bench.

Armed with black trash bags (she hated to think of Vivienne's things as trash), Calista began removing clothes from hangers and placing them in the bag. The clothes smelled like Vivienne. Like perfume she used to wear. Tears glistened in Calista's eyes as she breathed in that familiar smell. Vivienne made the ultimate sacrifice for her baby. Now she was gone. Calista wiped her eyes. She wished she would've called one of the girls to help her with this. It was a lot harder than she thought it would be. But she had to do it. Garrison certainly couldn't.

THIRTY MINUTES INTO it, she slowed down,

paced herself. She took her time putting Vivienne's clothes in bags. Then she moved on to her shoes. Purses. Belts.

"I don't know if you would even want to take something, but you're welcome to."

Calista turned around at the sound of Garrison's voice. He was leaning against the door frame with his arms crossed. With a rapidly beating heart, she said, "You startled me."

"Sorry."

"I thought you'd left."

"No, I was doing some work outside to get my mind off of things, you know."

"Oh," Calista said. "And I don't want to take any of Vivienne's things. It'll only make me sadder." Calista took a good long look at Garrison. Sadness glinted in his eyes. She didn't have to wonder how he was feeling tonight. He'd been testy since she arrived. And standing at the door, watching her pack up Vivienne's wardrobe would only make his mood worsen. And how long had he been standing there anyway? However long, it wasn't good for him to watch this. He needed to go back downstairs or outside. He needed to be somewhere else besides here.

Garrison took a few steps into the closet, sat down on the bench and hung his head.

"Gary, I can handle things here. I know you probably don't—"

"I'm fine, Calista." He looked up, noticing five bags lined up in front of where Vivienne's clothes used to hang. He rubbed his hands together before burying his face in them.

Calista swallowed hard. "Gary." She dropped the bag she had in her hand and walked over to the bench to sit next to him. "Gary, why don't you go back downstairs and let me take care of this, okay?"

He didn't respond. Didn't move.

"Gary."

He lowered his hands, looked at her and that's when she saw his eyes brimming with tears. He couldn't hold them in any longer. He tried. He failed.

"I'm so sorry, Gary," Calista said, batting her own tears away. She needed to be strong to support him right now.

Garrison shook his head. He slumped down, covered his face with his hands again while his elbows rested on his knees.

Calista scooted closer to him, wrapped her arms around him as best as she could. "I know this is difficult, and it's okay to cry, Gary," she said, feeling his body tremble against hers. And he sniffled. He didn't whimper and he wasn't audibly crying. He just sniffled.

And Calista held him, not knowing what to say to console him at this point, so she comforted him with her embrace while wishing he would've stayed outside. At least, then, he wouldn't be staring at Vivienne's clothes, reinforcing in his mind that this really was it – Vivienne wasn't coming back.

She moved her arms away from him when she felt him about to stand. And he did. He stood up, tall. She joined him.

"Gary, I'll finish everything up in here. Why don't you go get some water or something?"

"No. I'm going to take these bags outside."

"Gary, I'll get those."

"No! I got 'em," he said picking up the bags and heading for the door.

"Gary, wait."

He stopped in the bedroom only a few steps away from the door, holding both bags in his hand. "What?"

"Please put the bags down and let me take care of making sure the clothes get to the donation center. I told you I would. Please?"

"No!" he yelled. "I don't want anyone wearing her clothes. I'm throwing them in the garbage."

"O-okay, if that's what you want, fine, but let me do it for you, Gary. You're in no condition to—" she stopped speaking when she watched him drop the bags and stare at her with a hard, penetrating gaze.

"What condition am I supposed to be in, Cali? I have a dead wife and a baby with no mother," he said with bitterness in his voice. "Tell me how I'm supposed to feel!"

"I can't tell you how to feel, Gary," Calista said with a softened voice, "But what I can tell you is, you've been trying to handle all of this by yourself. You haven't been to any family dinners—"

"And neither have you," he interrupted to say.

He had her there. She hadn't been to any family dinners, but that was all because of

Barringer. She didn't want to run into him. "Yes, but that's a different situation. You know Barringer and I have been going through some things."

His forehead creased. "And I'm not?"

"You are. I'm not implying that you're not. I know how much you...I know you're hurting. I realize that, okay. I spend more time with you than anyone else in this family. You hardly talk to your brothers. Your mother, bless her heart, has been trying to get you over to her house for last month's family dinners and you refused to go. What is it, Gary? Tell me what makes you shut out everyone who loves you because of this...this tragedy?" Calista exhaled sharply. "And I'm sorry I have to raise my voice, but you don't understand, apparently, and I'm tired of watching you destroy yourself."

A wry smile touched his lips. "Now I remember why we broke up in college. You and that smart mouth of yours. Constantly talking and have no idea what you're talking about?"

Calista frowned. "You want to go there. Okay. We broke up because of your roving eyes, Gary, but that's besides—"

"Roving eyes," he interjected with dents in his forehead as he stepped closer to her.

"Yes," Calista said. "Roving eyes. I heard the rumors...tried to ignore them because I loved you, at the time, but when your best friend tells you that your man was trying to get with her, it's pretty hard to ignore, don't you think?"

He smirked. "You mean your best friend, Trinity. Your best friend who tried to come on to me. Your best friend who I sent away, told her she should be ashamed of herself for claiming to be your friend while, at the same time, trying to get with me. That friend?"

Calista looked stunned. "What?"

"She was trying to get at me, Calista. Of course she made up lies on me, and you fell for it. I wasn't with anyone else in college. I loved you. When we broke up...when you broke up with me, it hurt. I almost failed that year because of it."

Calista massaged her temples. She couldn't believe what she was hearing. Her friend Trinity had lied. And they weren't even friends anymore. They lost contact after college, but the fact remains that, now, Calista knew the girl had lied on Garrison. He'd never cheated on her. "You know what, Gary," she said in a frustrated breath, "You can do whatever you want with Vivienne's things. I'm going to go."

Calista headed for the door, but Garrison held out his arm, blocking her from walking by. She looked at him.

"You don't think you owe me an apology?" he asked her.

"Apology for what? Something that happened eleven years ago?"

"So what? It was eleven years ago. You said you were tired of watching me *destroy* myself, right?"

"Gary—"

"Right?" he asked again. "If that's the case, why not help me put the pieces of my life back together, Cali?"

Calista looked up at him, into his dark brown eyes – eyes identical to Barringer's. Tears swam in them. She felt her breath catch when he placed his large hands beside her face.

"I'm sorry, Gary," she said sadly.

"Okay, Calista. And for the record, I did love you. I'm sorry you thought otherwise, but I did love you. I still do, as my sister-in-law. And you're right about me. I *am* struggling. You're one hundred percent correct. I do need my family, but I don't know how to let them in without completely falling apart."

"You have to fall apart, if necessary. You have to let them see your pain, Gary."

A tear escaped his eye and rolled down the length his face. "Then I guess I have to give you the same advice," he said as she brushed the tear away from his face. "My brother really loves you, Cali. I know Barry can be arrogant and flashy and he gets on everybody's nerves," Garrison said with a slight grin, "But he loves you."

Tears formed in her eyes as she thought about Barringer now. He had confessed to her that he couldn't have babies. She wondered if Garrison knew, but she was too upset to ask. Instead, she cried while Garrison pulled her into his embrace, holding her head firmly against his chest. And she cried all she wanted to. She cried for Vivienne. For Junior. Cried for hurting Garrison all those years ago. Cried for Barringer who must've been in more pain than she was in. It must've taken a lot of courage for Barringer to admit the wrong he'd done. But he had, and she kicked him out – hadn't said a word to him since.

Calista broke their embrace by pulling away from Garrison. "I should probably go."

"No, don't go," Garrison said.

Calista wiped her eyes with the bend of her thumbs.

"I need you to help me," he said.

"I packed up all the clothes, Gary."

"I know. I mean with the pictures. Can you help me take them down while I still have the nerve to do it?"

Calista nodded, just barely. "Yes. I'll help you."

Chapter 22

"Good morning," Garrison said, stepping into the kitchen.

He had convinced Calista to spend the night in one of the guest bedrooms since they worked well past midnight. They'd managed to get all the pictures from the walls and packed up in boxes that he placed in the garage.

"Good morning," Calista said. She was busy cooking eggs and frying bacon. "Hope we didn't wake you. Since your son loves my singing, I had to sing for him this morning."

Garrison grinned. "Sure you did."

Calista laughed.

"No, you didn't wake me. The smell of bacon woke me. You know Vivienne had a thing about greasy smells when she was pregnant, so the smell of fried meat has me high right now."

"And how did you sleep?" she asked since last night was the first night he'd slept in the master bedroom since Vivienne's passing.

"I slept better than I've slept in a long time. I didn't think I would, but I did. Thank you for talking me into it."

"You're welcome." She watched him sit on a barstool. "Do you want milk or juice?"

"I'll get it, Cali. You're not a maid."

Calista smiled. "No, sit. I don't mind."

"All right, then. I'll take some juice if there's some in there. I've never been much of a grocery shopper. Vivienne always took care of that."

"Are you telling me you don't know how to buy your own food, Garrison Blackstone?"

He smiled. "I know how to, but I don't prefer to. Besides, you ladies know where everything is. I go in a grocery store and end up spending three-hundred dollars for what you could get for a hundred."

Calista chuckled. "Yep, you're a Blackstone all right. Barringer always picks up the most expensive items. And forget about using a coupon. I had a coupon for fifty cents off a box of cereal and he looked at me like I had personally offended him. Needless to say that was the last time we've ever shopped for groceries together."

Garrison laughed, watching her take a glass and open the refrigerator. His eyes widened when he saw that it was full. Well-stocked. "You bought food?" he asked her.

"Yes."

"When?"

"Earlier. Me and Junior were already up, so we went on a little grocery-shopping excursion.

Stocked the pantry too. Oh, and I sorted through everything in the fridge and pantry...threw out all the expired items." She walked over to him and set the glass of orange juice down in front of him.

"Thank you for this, for everything," Garrison said, and he meant it.

"You're welcome, Gary."

He watched her walk over to the stove thinking his brother was a lucky man. He didn't know how good of a woman he had. Or maybe he did. Whatever the case, Barringer didn't seem like he was fighting hard enough for her. He was allowing things to go on as is.

"So how has junior been this morning?"

"He's been okay. He's such a good baby...must've gotten that from his mother."

"Ouch," Garrison smirked.

Calista prepared a plate of eggs, bacon and toast, took it to island where he was sitting, then prepared a plate for herself. She sat next to him where they both had a good view of Junior in his baby swing, sleeping soundly.

"When was the last time you talked to Barry, Calista?" Garrison asked before biting into a piece of toast.

"When was the last time *you* talked to Barry, Gary?" Calista shot back.

They both grinned.

"I asked you first," Garrison said.

"Okay. I talked to him yesterday."

"Oh, yeah? That's an improvement."

"Not really. He came to my place, unannounced, and invited himself in."

"Was he decked out? The man acts like wearing a pair of jeans is low class."

Calista chuckled. Garrison knew his brother well.

"Surprisingly, he was wearing a baseball cap, a white T-shirt and blue jeans."

Garrison's eyebrows lifted.

"I know. Stranger things have happened, right?"

"No. I think this one takes the cake." Garrison laughed.

So did she. "Anyway, he wanted to apologize that he couldn't..."

"Couldn't what, Cali?"

She took a sip of juice and turned to the left to look at Garrison. "Did you know?"

"Did I know what?"

"That Barringer couldn't have children. I know he told you guys."

"I found out recently."

Calista scrunched up her face while she watched Garrison stuff eggs inside his mouth. "You found out recently?"

"Yeah. Why?"

"Because he knew about his *problem* before we were married. He's known all along. That's what he came by to tell me yesterday. That's what he apologized for. Said he tried to fix the situation, but nothing worked. Needless to say I broke down and cried. I was so upset, Gary. I still can't believe he kept that from me after five years. He just kept on stringing me along, letting me believe we would have a family one day and it was all a lie."

"Not all of it."

"What do you mean?"

"My brother genuinely loves you, Cali."

"You do realize you told me the same thing last night."

"I know, and I'm saying it again. He loves you. Nobody thought Barringer would even get married. Then he met you. If he could give you a baby, he would. Now, I guess you have to ask yourself if you married him for a baby, or because you loved him and wanted to be with him through thick and thin. Better or worse."

"Jeez...now you sound like Colton."

"Who?" Garrison asked, frowning. "Did you say Colton?"

Calista laughed.

"I know Colton didn't try to give you any advice."

"He did," Calista said once she could stop laughing. "He's so grumpy, I was surprised he had anything to say at all."

"Well, if Colton is trying to get you and Barringer back together, by all means, call Barringer right now." Garrison chuckled. "Seriously, though, Cali. Five years of marriage is worth fighting for, even if things didn't work out the way you planned."

"Yeah..." Calista said unenthused.

"That didn't sound believable."

She looked at him. "Because I hate that he kept it from me, Garrison. If he could hide something as serious as this, what else could he be hiding?"

"I don't think he's hiding anything, but what

I do know is, you owe my brother a sit-down, one-on-one conversation. Think about how he must feel about the situation. To carry on their legacy is a big deal to men and he can't do that. He needs your support. Don't make the same mistake you made with us. Had you come to me and talked about what you *thought* I was doing behind your back, who knows where our relationship could've gone. Talk to him."

"Okay. I'll talk to him, but only if you agree to come to the next family dinner."

"Where at?"

"Everson and June's house. This Saturday."

"Okay, so that gives you four days to talk to Barringer."

"I can do that."

"And you have to come to the family dinner, too."

She grinned. "I thought my attendance was implied."

"Okay. Let's shake on it," Garrison said, reaching for her hand.

"Seriously?"

"Yep."

Calista took his hand into hers and squeezed. "Deal." When he released her hand, she took a bite of bacon. "So, what are your plans for the day?" she asked, chewing.

"I thought I would go up to BFSG and see everybody."

"By everybody, you mean Barringer and Candice?"

Garrison grinned. "BFSG employs a lot of people, Cali."

"I know...didn't know you were friends with them all, though."

"Not friends, per se. Associates. I had a good rapport with the employees, especially the ones who reported directly to me."

"So you're going back for a visit. That's a good sign."

"Good sign of what?"

"That you may want your old job back."

"I thought about it."

"And?"

"Haven't made up my mind."

"So you're going to make up your mind on your drive over?"

He looked at her. "Not sure yet, Cali. And why do you want me to go back so badly anyway?"

"I told you...I think it'll help you get back into the swing of things. It'll be good for you. Plus, Barringer is having a hard time. I'm sure he can use your help, even though he would never admit it."

"Aw, see, look at you trying to help Barry."

Calista beamed. "Anyway, I'm meeting the ladies for lunch today, or I should say, Junior is meeting the ladies for lunch. They melt when they see him...another reason you need to work your way back into associating with the family again. They all love the first little Blackstone baby."

"Yeah. I see that now." Garrison finished his orange juice. "Breakfast was delicious. Thank you."

"You're welcome," she said, holding his

vision, looking away when it became awkward.

She stood up, scooped up their dishes and said, "I have to get going...need to run back home and take care of some things."

"Okay," Garrison said standing. "I'm going to head upstairs and get dressed. You'll probably be gone when I get back, so..." He walked over to Junior, left a kiss on his cheek and whispered, "I love you, son."

And when he stood upright again, he walked over to Calista and surprised her with a bear hug. "Thank you, Cali."

Calista closed her eyes. She remembered when she used to get similar, meaningful hugs from Barringer. "You're welcome, Gary." She felt his arms constrict tighter around her. "Any tighter and I won't be able to breathe," she managed to say.

He released her. "I just want you to know how much I appreciate you."

"Trust me, I know."

Garrison left a kiss at her temple. "I'll come by the apartment and pick up Junior later."

"Okay. Try to enjoy yourself today, Gary," Calista turned to him to say.

"I will," he said, then sauntered towards the stairs.

Chapter 23

Garrison stepped in the building, taking the elevator up to the fourth floor. He spoke to a few people on the way up and now, breezing by his old office, he headed to Barringer's office.

He tapped on the door then proceeded inside, not waiting for an answer.

Barringer was on a call. He held up an index finger, signaling to Garrison that he was almost done.

Garrison grinned silently. Barringer was dressed sharp, in a gray suit and grey and white striped shirt. When Garrison was working there, he instituted casual Fridays and NFL jersey Mondays, but his brother never took part in it. He was stern, set in his ways.

Barringer hung up the phone, leaned back in his chair with his hands behind his head and said, "I see you dusted off a suit, Gary. What brings you by?"

Garrison shook his head, sliding his hands

inside of his pockets. "Still upset I quit, huh?"

"That among other things," Barringer said, looking at his computer screen, scanning through an email from Eleanor, keying a quick reply.

"What other things, Barry?"

Barringer shrugged his large shoulders while still typing. After sending the email, he looked up at Garrison and said, "You know. Things. Like the amount of time you've been spending with my wife."

A frown appeared in Garrison's forehead. "*Your* wife has been helping me with my son."

A creepy, borderline evil smile appeared on Barringer's face. "Funny how life happens. I can't give my wife a baby, but my brother can."

Garrison glared at his brother. Usually levelheaded, he couldn't help the frown that deepened and tightened in his forehead along with the merciless throbbing at his temples. "Calista has been there for me. She takes care of Junior."

"What else is she doing, Gary?" Barringer asked in an accusatory tone.

Garrison narrowed his eyes. "What are you implying?"

"You've been playing house with my wife for the last three months."

"Playing house? Calista has been taking care of my son. How many times have you seen Junior since leaving the hospital, Barringer? How many? I'll tell you...none. How many times have you called me to see how I was doing because *I* lost my wife? How many?

None!"

"That's a lie. I called you once. You didn't answer the phone."

"Once? Yeah, thanks. I appreciate the effort," Garrison said with sarcasm in his voice. "You're my brother, my flesh and blood, and you're so hardhearted, you can't understand how anyone else feels about anything. Everything is about you."

Barringer rose to his feet. "Man, get out of my office. I don't have time for this."

"Everyone calls me except you. I may not answer the phone all the time, but it's nice to know people care. But you…you call *one* time and take it as a personal insult that I didn't answer. You could've come by the house. It's not like you don't know where I live. You could visit your nephew every once in a while."

Garrison shook his head and continued, "I thought I would come here today and request my job back, but now I see it's not what I want. I can't work with you anymore, man."

"Then don't," Barringer said with anger.

Garrison blew a breath before he left Barringer's office. Deciding not to make his trip a complete waste, he walked down the hallway and chatted with some of his former employees. It would've been nice to see Candice, but he knew she was out to lunch with the womenfolk today.

* * *

The women sat around a round table,

looking at menus and sipping on ice water. The sun, encased in a bright, blue sky, made their midday lunch getaway even more enjoyable. More exciting. When was the last time the ladies got together like this?

Instead of looking at the menu, Candice was speaking 'baby' to little Junior, bouncing him and smelling him. "Oh, babies smell so good."

Calista smiled. "They do. I love smelling him. And I love the fact that he's Vivienne's. Makes me want to take extra special care of him like she wanted."

Kalina nodded. "Hey, Cali, have you spoken to Barringer yet?"

"He came by the apartment, and yes. He told me. I know you already know what I'm talking about."

Kalina nodded. June took a sip of water. Of course they knew, being married to Barringer's brothers.

"Well, I don't know. What's going on?" Candice asked. Seemed she was the only one out of the loop.

"Um...well, turns out, Barringer and I couldn't have a baby anyway."

Candice's forehead creased. "Why not?"

"He's sterile."

"Oh my gosh," Candice said. "Poor Barringer."

The waitress came by, took food orders, then quickly left.

Junior began wiggling and squirming in Candice's lap before a faint cry ensued.

"Okay, this is where I hand him back to you,

Cali," Candice said.

Once Junior settled in Calista's arms, he calmed down. Calista took a bottle from the diaper bag and watched Junior clamor for it. "Goodness, lil' man. You're that hungry?" she asked him.

"You're a natural," June told her. "I know Garrison appreciates you being able to take care of Junior like this."

"He does...tells me all the time."

Kalina frowned, quickly removing the disturbance from her forehead when Calista saw her.

"What is it, Kalina?" Calista asked. "You looked like you wanted to say something."

"I was wondering how Barringer feels about all this. I mean, here it stands, he can't give you a baby, but you're taking care of his brother's baby."

"I don't know how Barringer feels about anything. Whenever I talk to him, he's insulting and rude...talks to me condescendingly like *I* did *him* wrong."

"But you can't ignore him forever," Candice said.

"I know, Candy. I'm going to talk to him soon. I just need time to process the fact that he lied to me."

"Well, technically, he didn't lie," June said. "He just didn't tell you."

"Same thing," Calista said. "He wasn't upfront with me."

"Would you still have married him if he had been?" June asked.

"Probably. I love Barry, but the last few years have been rough. He's always stressed out about the job. Ugh. I don't even want to talk about it. I'm beginning to sound like a broken record." Calista took a sip of juice. "No, I take that back. A broken record sounds better." She dug around in the diaper bag for a burp cloth. Junior had since gone to sleep and she needed to burp him before strapping him inside of the car seat. So, she threw the cloth over her left shoulder held Junior against her so his head rested on her shoulder and rubbed his back in circular motions.

"This is totally off topic, but I think Everson is cheating on me," June said.

"What?" Kalina, Calista and Candice all said together.

"No way," Candice said. "I know I sit here and have these girly pow-wows with y'all, but I grew up with these men. These are my brothers we're talking about."

"I realize that, Candy."

"Then you know Everson wouldn't cheat on you," Candice said in Everson's defense.

June shrugged. "He's always on the phone. Always gone, and I usually travel with him but for the last couple of months, he's been requesting to travel alone. Even when I tell him I want to go, he finds a reason why I shouldn't."

"Well, if you knew him like I knew him, you know he wouldn't do that to you," Candice said. "Seriously, June? As much as Everson wanted you? Yeah, he tried to be a player back in the day. Shoot, they all were, well except for

Bryson. He was more conservative."

Kalina smiled.

"And Garrison even went to the left for a while there after some woman broke his heart in college," Candice said.

Calista's heart almost stopped beating when Candice brought that up.

"But still, when they commit, they commit," Candice said.

The waitress brought the food by.

"And as for you, Cali," Candice continued, "Don't act like you didn't know how Barringer was before y'all were married. He's always been short-tempered. Expects everything to go his way. The fact that he can't give you a baby is killing him. You should see him at the office. He can't concentrate on a thing. In meetings, he looks like a...like an android. I can't even talk to him half the time without wanting to slap him across the head, but I hang in there because I know sometimes his sarcasm and rudeness is a cry for help. And to Kalina's point, how do you think it makes him feel to see you with a baby knowing he can't give you a baby. It must hurt. Barringer has too much pride. I doubt if he would ever admit it, but put yourself in his shoes. It must be a thorn in his flesh to see you taking care of another man's baby, even if it is his brother's child."

Calista lowered Junior into his car seat and strapped him in. Then she began eating her salad. She didn't respond to Candice because what else was there to say?

AFTER LUNCH, THE women took a stroll on the Riverwalk before preparing to go their separate ways. Hugs were exchanged. Kisses were left all over a sleeping Junior.

"Don't forget...family dinner at my house on Saturday," June reminded them.

"Got it," Kalina said.

Everyone dispersed, heading to their vehicles.

"Hey, Candy, wait up," Calista said, pushing the stroller faster to catch up to Candice.

Candice stopped, turned around and said, "Hey, what's up?"

"You know, don't you?"

"That's sort of an open-ended question, but if you're talking about the fact that you and Garrison used to be an item in college, yes, I know. I also know you're the one who broke his heart, Cali. Vivienne told me a long time ago about you and Garrison...don't know why you wanted to keep it a secret."

"For obvious reasons. As you yourself said, Barringer is short-tempered. Imagine how far to the left he'll go if he finds out about me and Garrison."

"But that's the thing, Cali...he's *going* to find out, especially now."

"How?"

"Don't know. I certainly won't say anything."

Calista sighed heavily.

"Look, Cali...I know you're helping Vivienne and I know Garrison needs you right now, but you need to be careful."

"Be careful? What are you talking about?"

"I'm talking about you and Garrison. Y'all have a history. And Garrison is the complete opposite of Barringer. I know. I grew up with them. Garrison is charming. Sweet. He's not a hothead." Candice grinned. "Basically, Garrison a better version of Barringer. I'm sure you're aware of that. Don't spend a lot of unnecessary time alone with Garrison. If your intention is to get back with Barringer, work towards that goal."

Calista turned her head to look out into the water while a breeze tackled her hair.

"Wait...is it your intention to get back with Barringer?" Candice asked.

Calista shrugged. "I'm not sure."

Candice frowned. "Cali—"

"I'm being honest, Candy. I'm not sure. What I am sure about is, I have no feelings for Garrison. I love him as my brother-in-law, the same way I love you as my sister-in-law."

"But you don't love Barry anymore?"

"I didn't say that. I—I don't know how to feel about Barry right now."

"Well, just be careful."

"Don't worry. I will."

Candice closed her arms around Calista, "See you later."

"Yep. Later."

Chapter 24

Calista had been home for a few hours, catching up on TV shows she'd recorded in the previous weeks. Junior wasn't sleeping tonight. Going into month four, he seemed extra alert. He made those sweet baby noises, stared at her and smiled while kicking and wiggling his little body.

Staring at the TV, Calista said, "He doesn't know it yet, but he's about to get ambushed, Junior."

Junior smiled as if he knew what Calista was saying.

"Are you smiling at me handsome boy?" she asked, watching a big gummy, slobbery smile brighten his face. When Calista heard the doorbell, she kissed Junior on the cheek and said, "Looks like daddy's here." She stood up with the baby in her arms, making her way to the door. "Let's see who it is." She took a quick glance in the peephole. "It *is* daddy."

Calista opened door. "Hey."

"Hey, Cali." He reached for his son, kissed him on the forehead, then stepped inside.

Calista closed the door. When she turned around, she looked him up and down. He was wearing a white T-shirt and a pair of light gray sweatpants. *I know he didn't wear that to the office. Or maybe he'd since changed clothes.* "How did it go today?"

"Not so good," Garrison said, taking a seat on the couch with Junior in his lap.

Calista thought he would pick up Junior and leave, but he was getting comfortable on the couch. *Okay, so he wants to talk.* "Can I get you something to drink?"

"No. I'm not staying. I know you need your personal time and I don't want to impose."

Calista thought about the talk she had with Candice, about not getting too close to Garrison, but she couldn't send him away, so she replied, "You're not imposing. What happened?"

"I told you I was going to the office today."

"Right," she said sitting next to him, touching Junior's hand, allowing him to wrap his little fingers around her index finger.

"And I spoke with Barringer, but he was belligerent. I've never seen Barry like that before."

"So let me guess...you decided you didn't want to go back to work there?"

"I wanted to go back. I know he needs help, but he just makes me want to choke him sometimes."

Calista laughed. "That's Barringer all right."

"I was so irritated, I told him I wasn't coming back. I'll find something else to do with my skills."

"What did you do for BFSG?"

"I headed up the finance division...basically I did forecasts, long and short-term financial planning, performance reporting, accounting, etcetera."

Calista smiled. Impressed.

"Why are you smiling?" he asked her.

"I just remembered you were always good with numbers," she said, still playing with Junior.

"I think you should talk to him, Cali. He's not well. He needs you."

"I was planning on calling him tonight, so—"

"Okay. Well, I'm going to get out of your hair so you can do that." Garrison stood up and lowered Junior into his car seat. "Thank you again, Cali."

"You're welcome. Hey, what time will you be by in the morning?"

"Oh, that's what I meant to tell you. "I'm going by my parent's house tomorrow. Mom feels slighted that I haven't been allowing her to keep Junior, but I wasn't ready to face them, you know. I figure I'd go by there tomorrow to smooth things over to avoid a confrontation at dinner on Saturday."

"Smart thinking."

"And you call your husband. He's driving everybody insane."

Calista smiled as she opened the door. "Pray

for me."

Garrison grinned. "All right, sis. I'll see you Saturday."

"Okay. Bye Junior."

* * *

Even though she was temporarily distracted by TV shows, she still had time to think about and meditate on what Candice had told her about Barringer. She said it must've been difficult for Barringer to watch her with Junior, all the while knowing he couldn't give her a child. Okay, she could see how that could be difficult, but it's not like she was intentionally trying to hurt Barringer.

And then there was what Candice said about Garrison. She warned Calista not to get too close to him because they used to date back in college. But that didn't mean they had feelings for each other now. He just lost his wife. Then again, there were those few occasions when they would hold each other a little longer when they embraced, or when he would leave a kiss at her temple. And when they would lock eyes in the midst of awkward silence.

Calista shook her head. She picked up her cell phone from the nightstand. She hadn't programmed Barringer's number into her new phone yet but she knew his number by heart. She dialed it and waited. And waited. And...

"Hello."

"Hi, Barry. It's—"

"I know your voice, Calista. We've been

married for five years, not that it means anything to you."

Calista shook her head. Barringer was already starting out wrong. *Why am I even trying*? "Barry, I didn't call you to argue."

"So why *did* you call me?"

Calista glanced at the clock. It was a few minutes after nine, and she could hear Barringer typing. He was still at the office. He could've been home on his laptop, but she doubted it.

"Hello?" he said. More like yelled.

"Are you still at work?"

"What's it to you?"

"Jeez, Barringer. Can't we have a simple conversation without you being rude?"

The line went quiet.

I know this man did not hang up on me...

"Barry?"

"A few days ago, I came to you, confessed to you, bared my soul to you about something that has plagued me for years and you sent me away."

"I sent you away because you lied to me, Barringer. You planned out all of this behind my back."

"Planned what out?" he hissed.

"Your life. This marriage. You knew you couldn't have children, but you wanted me, so screw what I wanted, right, because Barringer does whatever pleases Barringer."

"That's not true."

"It *is* true. You never discuss anything with me. Sometimes I feel like I need to make an appointment with you just so you can talk to me."

Barringer released a frustrated breath. "I don't know what you want right now. What do you want from me, Calista? You've been gone for a little over three months now. What do you want?"

"I want to know why you lied to me."

"I didn't lie. I—"

"I want to know why you didn't tell me about your *situation* before we married, Barringer. When we were dating, we talked all the time. I shut people out of my life so I could devote all of my time to you. And you did the same for me. We talked. We did everything together. We talked about a family. I told you I wanted kids. We were supposed to spend the first two years of our marriage getting to know each other on a deeper level, remember? The kids would come after we grew closer. Did we not discuss that?"

"We did."

"Then you very easily could've told me you were sterile. Instead, you made the decision to marry me and not tell me a thing. You kept this secret for over six years. You entered into a marriage with me carrying this secret. How...how am I supposed to trust you now? How?"

The line went quiet again. Calista knew he was still there. The call was still connected and she could hear him breathing.

"I don't know, Calista. But, as I told you before, I thought I could go see a doctor and get my issues resolved without having to involve you. You think I didn't want to give you a baby?"

"Yes. That's what I thought because that's what you led me to believe. Any time the topic of a baby would come up, you said it wasn't the right time. Said we needed to wait another year, or you were too busy on the job to bring a child into the world. Always an excuse, but now I understand they were lies."

Again, silence.

"So where do we go from here?" he asked.

"I don't know. I honestly don't. Maybe..." Calista wanted to suggest marriage counseling, but she wasn't sure if it could help their situation. "I'm going to bed." *Alone, just like when I was living with you.* She thought it, but didn't say it. She had told him to chill with the sarcasm, so she had to do the same. "Bye, Barringer."

She ended the call before waiting to see if he would respond back. "What am I going to do?" This situation was driving her crazy. There had to be a resolution but what? She picked up the phone and decided to send Kalina a message:

Calista: Hey, I need to talk to you about something. Can we meet in the morning?

She glanced at her toenails and wiggled her toes while waiting for Kalina to respond back. A good day of pampering would surely take her mind off of Barringer.

Kalina: Sure. Can you meet me at Edith's Café, say around 9?

Calista smiled as she responded back:

Calista: Yes. See you then.

She placed her phone on the nightstand, turned off the lamp and laid there in bed staring at the TV, but not watching it. She thought about her issues – about Barringer. He didn't seem like himself anymore. And now, she wondered if their marriage was worth the effort or if they should remain apart. Something had to be done. When a married man wanted to live as if he was single, what was the point of getting married? Then there was the secret he'd kept from her...

Calista grabbed the remote and shut off the TV. Her head pounded with various thoughts running through her mind while tears came to her eyes. She closed her eyes, forced them away and willed herself to sleep.

Chapter 25

"Mr. Champion is here with a Mr. Hempstead, sir," Eleanor said via intercom to Barringer. Should I have them sent up?"

"Please," Barringer responded. He left his office and sauntered to the conference room where Candice was already waiting with her laptop.

"Is he here yet?" she asked Barringer as soon as he opened the door with his tablet tucked underneath his left arm and a cup of coffee in his left hand.

"Just got here. I told Eleanor to send them on up."

Candice raised her brows. "Them?"

"Yeah. He brought somebody with him."

"Hmm...this should be interesting," Candice said.

"And remember, we're not making any final decisions, Candy. We just want to hear what they have to say."

"I know. I wish Garrison was here with us," she pouted.

"Garrison has more important things to do," he said bitterly.

"Barry, you do know it's okay to have a life outside of work. Garrison is going through a rough time right now."

"Yeah. Sure. Whatever."

Candice frowned, but she quickly straightened her face when she saw the men approaching the door.

She stood up, so did Barringer, but when her eyes caught sight of one of the men, Kurt Hempstead, she felt the blood completely drain out of her face. Before she could stop herself, she asked, "What are you doing here?"

Desmond looked at Candice, then glanced at Kurt.

Barringer looked at Candice.

Kurt's lips curved into a smile when he asked, "What are *you* doing here?"

"I take it you two know each other," Desmond said.

"Uh...n-no. Not really," Candice stammered.

Kurt cracked a half smile.

"Well, just for formalities, hi, I'm Desmond Champion, director of marketing and business relations at The Champion Corporation." He extended his hand to Candice.

"Nice to meet you Mr. Champion," she said, accepting his hand. "I'm Candice Blackstone, customer relations manager at BFSG."

"Pleased to meet you, and please call me Desmond."

"And I'm Kurt Hempstead, marketing manager at The Champion Corporation." He reached to shake Candice's hand. She welcomed his hand into hers, squeezing hard, giving him a good business handshake. Now she knew what the letters TCC, on the business card he'd given her, stood for.

Barringer introduced himself as BFSG's CEO, greeting the men with a handshake. "Have a seat, gentleman," he told them.

The men sat down, Kurt taking the seat directly across from Candice.

"I have to say I was a little surprised you agreed to take a flight here to meet with us," Barringer said, looking at Desmond.

"Actually, I didn't fly," Desmond said. "I drove. Just so happens me and my wife are on a little vacation getaway from the kids. Twins. Girl and a boy."

"Aw...how old," Candice asked.

"They're three months." He fished his wallet from his back pocket and took out a family picture.

Candice's mouth fell open. "Oh my goodness...it's a small world." She looked up at Desmond. "Sherita's your wife?"

Desmond smiled. "Yes. You know her?"

"Do I *know* her? We used to cheer together in high school! And look at these beautiful little babies. They are adorable."

"Thank you."

Candice glanced over at Barringer, seeing his straight, annoyed face. She handed the picture back to Desmond.

"And how do you and Kurt know each other?" Desmond asked.

"We don't know each other," Kurt said. "Just bumped into one another on the Riverwalk a while ago."

"Interesting," Desmond said. "Well, since the ice has been broken, I guess we can get down to business."

"Yes," Barringer said. "Let's talk Blakeney."

"Actually, that's not the reason I'm here."

"It's not?"

"No. While BFSG used to handle the financial services for The Blakeney Agency, now they're our client. Therefore, I cannot discuss privileged information with you."

Barringer leaned back in his seat, annoyed. "The Blakeney Agency has been with BFSG for over two decades."

"Yes, thank you for that, but I've done my research. I'm aware The Blakeney Agency was a deal your father, Mr. Theodore Blackstone, secured. Times have changed, Barringer. More and more companies are looking for ways to streamline their financial services under one umbrella. One company. That's what we do at The Champion Corporation. We take care of all of our client's financial services from payroll to forecasting, and when the financial outlook of one of our clients seems bleak, we offer marketing services to help them boost their bottom line."

"Wait," Candice said. "So let me understand."

"Sure," Desmond said, interlocking his

fingers, resting his hands on the table.

"So you provide payroll services to all of your clients?"

"Yes. We have a payroll division within our accounting and finance department, headed up by my brother, Dimitrius Champion. He's constantly developing new technologies to assist our clients with their financial needs."

"And you handle books, taxes, forecasting...?"

"We do. We see a client's profit margin slipping, we immediately call a meeting to notify them. If it becomes a trend, we devise marketing plans to reverse the downward spiral and increase profits to where it should be, even beyond where they were. That's where Kurt is usually focusing all of his time."

Candice glanced at Kurt, then back over to Desmond.

"So if you don't want to discuss The Blakeney Agency today, why did you agree to meet with us?" Barringer asked.

"Good question," Desmond said. "First, I want to say, despite whatever rumors you've heard, The Champion Corporation is not in the business of stealing our competitor's clients. It's only when clients come to us that we inform them what we have to offer. With that being said, I admire BFSG and the work you do. Your profits have been consistent year after year, but after losing a client as big as Blakeney, I'm sure that's going to change for you. So I have a proposition."

Barringer's brows snapped together. "A

proposition?"

"Yes," Kurt said. He took out a manila folder from his briefcase and handed everyone a pamphlet. "We've done a preliminary work-up on BFSG. Thirty-five percent of your client base is coming up on contract renewals within the next two years. Since most of them probably already know you lost The Blakeney Agency to TCC, we've been receiving quite a number of calls from your clients already, requesting information."

Desmond nodded. "We have meetings lined up all next week."

Barringer crossed his arms. Could things get any worse for him?

"But, we don't want to take your clients, Barringer," Desmond said. "We see this as an opportunity to work together."

"How's that?" Candice asked, sounding as confused as she looked.

"Presently, BFSG does something TCC does not."

"Which is?" Barringer said, sitting up straight again.

"Investment services. Believe it or not, it was the only reason The Blakeney Agency didn't want to leave BFSG, but after much negotiating, they reluctantly agreed to go without it. Since TCC doesn't have an investment division, we thought we could work together."

"How's that?" Candice inquired.

"Well, we're looking to expand in the next few years. As you know, we're based out of

Asheville, but it would be of much benefit to have a branch office in Wilmington."

"Okay, hold it right there," Barringer said. "If you're talking about trying to buy us out—"

"No, not at all, Barringer," Desmond said. "We want to work with you. We want to bring BFSG under the Champion brand. Now, it—"

"No way," Barringer interjected.

"Now, before you make a decision, I think it would be best if you read through the pamphlet."

"No. My father built this company from the ground up. I'll be a fool to let you and your brothers try to take it from me."

"Barringer, hold on a sec," Candice said.

"No. I'm not entertaining anymore of this." Barringer stood up. "This meeting is over."

Barringer stormed out of the room, pushing the door to the conference room to a slam.

"I'm sorry about that fellas," Candice said.

"No apology necessary. It was a pleasure to meet you, Candice. I'll be sure to tell my wife I ran into you." Desmond stood up.

"Please do," Candice said.

"Ready Kurt?" Desmond asked, when he noticed Kurt wasn't making an effort to get up. He was caught in a trance with Candice.

"Yeah," Kurt said, "But give me a minute."

"All right." Desmond exited the room, making his way down to the lobby.

"Is your brother always so hotheaded?" Kurt asked Candice.

"When he feels like he's being backed into a corner, he is. This company means the world to him."

"Which is the very reason he should take the deal. He should view this as a courtesy. The Champion brothers are usually more aggressive. I've seen them swallow up companies, their divisions and subsidiaries. This is the first time they've made an offer to make a company a division of TCC."

"Well, Barringer's the CEO. He makes the final decision, so—"

"How about we talk about this over drinks?" Kurt asked.

"How long are you in town?"

"How long do you need me to be in town?"

Candice failed to withhold a smile. She took a business card from the jacket of a blazer, scribbled her cell phone number on it before handing it to him. "Call me."

"Will do." He stood up and said, "It was nice seeing you again, by the way."

She smiled. "You as well. Have a good day, Kurt."

"Trust me. I will."

Chapter 26

"I think it's really over, Kalina," Calista said, holding a fresh cup of coffee. She took a sip.

"Why?"

"Because he's not himself anymore. I talked to him last night."

"Okay, and what happened?"

"The man I was on the phone with last night, briefly might I add, is not the man I married. He's insolent...we can't talk without arguing. I can't handle that."

"People handle stress in different ways. Bryson tells me Barringer has always been an overachiever."

Calista nodded. "He has. He likes a certain lifestyle, you know."

"Then he must be under a lot of stress right now."

"I'm sure he is, but that's no reason to throw things at me and think I should be okay with it."

Kalina frowned.

"I don't mean literally throw things at me, Kalina." Calista grinned.

"Oh. Shrew. You had me worried for a minute there."

"Barry would never hurt me, physically that is. What I mean is, he gives me things, hoping they will somehow compensate for him not being there for me. The first two years of our marriage, I thought it was his way of being generous and appreciative, you know, trying to be a good husband. Later, I realized I didn't have a husband. He was always gone."

Calista took a sip of coffee.

"Last night, he asked me where we go from here, and honestly, Kalina, I didn't know what to tell him. I feel like, if I move back home, everything will go right back to the way it was, and I don't want that anymore."

"What do you want?"

"I want a family man...a man who values his wife more than he does his work."

"But let's look at this realistically, Cali. A man has to work to take care of his family."

Calista nodded. "True. I definitely didn't want a non-working man, but when a man is more dedicated to his job than he is to his family, that's a problem. Look at you and Bryson. He owns a business. You own a business. Yet, you guys are happy. You make time for each other. I doubt if Bryson spends his nights at the office."

Kalina smiled. "No, he does not."

"Exactly," Calista said. "He makes time for

you because he values you. Barringer doesn't value me. If he did, he would've told me he was sterile before we married, right?"

"Maybe, but men are some prideful individuals. It has to be doing a number on him to know that the one thing you want, he can't give you. So in my mind, I'm thinking he has the right to ask you where the relationship is going, simply because the ball is in your court, sweetie."

"How's that?"

Kalina set her cup down in front of her and said, "Now that you know he can't have children, are you willing to love him anyway?"

Calista nodded, eyes flooded with tears. "Yes. Better or worse, right?"

Calista placed her cup on the table before quickly hiding her face with her hands.

"Oh, Cali, don't cry," Kalina said, standing up and pulling a chair next to Calista. She sat down, threw an arm around her. "It's going to be okay. Issues like this take a little more time to iron out, but it's going to be okay."

Calista's hands trembled as she cried. She moved them away from her face, then took a napkin to dab the corners of her eyes. "All I ever wanted was a simple, normal life. I don't ask for much. I hardly ask for anything." She sniffled, dabbed her nose. "I don't know what to do, Kalina."

"Well, first, you need to calm down a bit. I know what stress can do to a person, Calista. Please, just calm down and take some deep breaths."

"I'll try."

"I know this is stressful, but you need to take some time for yourself. I'm worried about you."

"I'll be okay. I've been feigning happiness for years."

"But—"

"I'll be fine." Calista sniffled, dabbing at her nose again. "I need to go." She stood up.

"Are you coming to the dinner tomorrow evening at June's?" Kalina asked.

"I don't know yet. I thought about it, but not sure if I can deal with Barringer right now."

"Okay." Kalina hugged Calista tight and held on. "Love you, sis."

"Love you, too, and don't worry about me, Kalina. I'll be fine. Okay."

"Okay. Just call me if you need me."

"I will."

Chapter 27

"Come on in, son," Theodore said after greeting Barringer with a hug. "Looks like we're getting all kind of surprises today, dear."

Elowyn came walking out of the kitchen with little Junior in her arms. "Well hello there, stranger."

Barringer cracked a smile. "Hello, mother." He walked up to her, leaned down to leave a kiss at her cheek. "How have you been, Barringer?"

"I'm okay."

"You look good," Elowyn said looking him up and down. "Dressed sharp."

"Thanks. I see Garrison has been by."

"Yes. He finally came to drop off little Junior. Finally! My prayers have been answered."

Barringer smirked. He knew how happy his parents were when they learned their first grandbaby was on the way. Too bad he wouldn't be able to give them any grandchildren.

"So what brings you by?" Theodore asked.

"I actually need to talk to you for a moment, Dad."

"Okay." He followed his father to the study, taking a seat in an old antique style chair. His father sat in the chair next to him.

"So, ah...I'm not sure how to say this so—"

"You want to talk to me about Blakeney. Am I right?" Theodore asked.

A look of surprise flushed over Barringer's face. "You know?"

The old man let out a rough chuckle. "Of course I know. I knew the same day it happened."

Confused, Barringer asked, "How?"

"Son, I still have eyes and ears all through the company. And I have a little secret weapon I like to refer to as daddy's angel."

"Candice."

Theodore laughed. "That Candice is something else. And you know what she said that really bothered me?"

"What's that?"

"She said, she wasn't worried about the company. She was worried about you."

"Dad—"

"Listen, Barry...I put in a few calls around to different companies. Blackstone Financial Services can't survive the loss of Blakeney. It just can't. Now, I heard about the meeting you had with The Champion Corporation, and after looking them up, son, the deal doesn't sound half bad."

Barringer frowned. "So you're giving up? Is that it? Or do you not have any faith in me to turn this company around?"

"I'm not giving up on you, Barringer, but it could take years to get a client like Blakeney. What's going to happen to the employees who depend on a paycheck week after week? I heard you were thinking about layoffs, but that's out of the question. Now, let's talk realistically here for a minute. I started this company. If I didn't have faith in you to run it, I wouldn't have made you CEO, son. I have faith in you, Barringer, to do the right thing, not for me. Not for your pride. Do it for the greater good...for the employees who are counting on you."

Barringer hung his head. His father was right. He couldn't dispute that.

"Who did you speak with from The Champion Corporation?"

"I had a meeting yesterday with Desmond Champion. Sounds like Candice has already filled you in, but anyway, he offered to make BFSG a division of their company. I told him I wouldn't do it. I'm not giving this company away."

"Who said anything about giving it away?"

"They're asking to make BFSG a part of The Champion Corporation which means they have to acquire BFSG," Barringer explained.

"Which, in turn, means they acquire debts and legal obligations and in most cases, all the employees. It's worth a real conversation, Barringer. One you should have with Candice and Garrison."

"Garrison," Barringer hissed. He stood up. "You know he quit. Did Candice tell you that?"

"No. Garrison told me he was thinking about taking a leave from the position. He had to get a lot of things in order in his life. Still doesn't mean he can't be a part of this conversation you need to have with Mr. Champion."

Barringer slid his hands in his pockets, pacing the floor in front of the bookshelves. "All right, Dad. I guess I have a lot of decisions ahead of me."

"You do, but take your time. Like I said, talk it over with Candice and Garrison."

"All right. I have to get back to the office."

"Okay. I'll see you at Everson's place tomorrow for dinner, right?"

"Yeah. I'll be there. Barringer left his father in the study and walked back to the living room where his mother looked like she'd been waiting for him. She was still holding a wide-awake Junior.

"Before you go, I want to ask you something, Barringer," Elowyn said.

He already knew what this would be about. "Yes, mother."

"What are you going to do to get Calista back?"

He blew a frustrated breath. "Mother, this is between me and Calista."

"I beg to differ," Elowyn said, raising her tone. "Son, we are a family. Calista has been my daughter-in-law for five years. You don't think I miss her. I love her, Barry, just like I love you and that woman has been good to you."

Barringer tempered his agitation by playing with the keys in the right pocket of his pants. "The situation is not easy, Mother. I lied to Calista. That's my fault. And quite honestly, I doubt if she wants me back. She wants a man who can give her a child, and she deserves that."

"Okay, so what are you going to do? Make a decision. You want to divorce her? You want to see her fall in love with another man and have *his* children? Can you imagine seeing her pregnant with another man's baby, Barringer?"

Barringer felt a sting in his heart just thinking about it. No, he couldn't imagine it. As much as he knew Calista deserved a man who could give her the kind of life she was seeking, he couldn't fathom her being touched by another man, let alone pregnant by one.

"Well?"

"No. I can't imagine that. Calista's mine. She always will be."

A smile came to Elowyn's face. She touched him on the forearm. "Glad to hear it. Hold on a second. I have something to give you."

She lowered Junior to his car seat. Standing upright again, Mama Blackstone wrapped her arms around Barringer.

Barringer, in turn, folded his arms around his mother whom he loved dearly.

"I know you're going through a storm right now, son," she said, "But you can handle it. You've never been a quitter. And please smile every once in a while, will you?"

"I will for you. I love you, Mother."

"I love you too, son."

"See you tomorrow, okay," she said, releasing him from her warm grasp.

"Looking forward to it already." With that, he headed for the door.

Chapter 28

No one could give him clarity like his mother. He considered himself fortunate to have a set of caring parents who loved him enough to tell him like it was, and Elowyn Blackstone had done just that. That's why, after finishing the work day, Barringer decided to pay Calista a visit, only to find she'd been leaving her apartment at seven in the evening. He wondered where she was going.

So he followed her.

She ended up at a bar not far from her apartment. Three or so miles down the street, maybe. Why was she at a bar? Was she meeting someone? He frowned, felt his blood sizzle at the thought of it as he shifted his car into park.

He watched Calista emerge from her car, her hair hanging loose. Looked like she'd added some curls to it. She wore a pair of sexy, black jeans that fit well on her hips and a thin, teal blouse. And she was at a bar like this? If her body didn't catch a man's attention, surely those pink, plump lips of hers would.

"Why are you at this bar, Cali?" Barringer asked quietly, watching her head for the entrance. She didn't go to bars. She didn't like bars. So why was she here?

Deciding to see for himself, he got out of his car, suit and all, stepping inside of the bar, careful to find her first, so he could find the perfect spot to sit and hide – one that would give him a good view of her without being exposed. He saw her sitting alone at a small table in the corner, so he went to the opposite corner and watched.

Calista took out her cell phone, probably checking messages, he guessed. A waitress brought her a glass of red wine. She loved red wine, he knew. Watching her take slow sips reminded him of all the times he'd come home from work to find out she'd cooked dinner. She usually cooked dinner when they weren't dining out. (And actually, he couldn't remember the last they'd done that.) And some of her dinners were special ones. She'd take the time to put a bottle of wine on ice, cook a gourmet meal, light candles, the whole nine – only to find out he couldn't make it. Or he'd tell her he'd be home, and something work-related would take precedence. Work always took precedence over her.

Now, his wife was sitting alone inside of a bar...

And he was watching every man in the place try to get her attention.

Why wouldn't they? Calista's intrinsic beauty was unmatched. He knew it, so why wouldn't other men notice? An additional thought hit him as he watched her lips part to take another sip of wine – when was the last time he told her she was beautiful?

Nearly six years into the marriage, he had been taking her for granted. He could see that as plain as day now. And Garrison was right. He couldn't blame other people for his problems. *He* lied to Calista. He appreciated people being open and honest with him, but he hadn't returned the favor. He could see how selfish he was now – how all of Calista's complaints were justified. And all those times she tried to leave before should've given him a clue that one day, she would find the courage to be gone for good.

Still, he didn't think she would actually do it. He gave her the ideal life. That's what women wanted right? Financial security, a fancy home – or so he thought. Calista didn't want those things. She only wanted him.

When he saw her look up and smile at someone approaching, he angled his head to get a view of whomever she was smiling at. It was a man, but he couldn't quite get a full view of him. A million knots formed in his stomach. Calista was meeting a man?

It was only when the man came into full view that Barringer felt like he'd lost the ability to breathe. The man who made his wife's face light up was none other than his own brother – Garrison Blackstone. Barringer balled fists.

Everything in him wanted to storm over there, catch them in the act and confront them both. Why were they meeting at a bar? Having drinks together? Laughing it up like they were best friends?

Instead of barging over to ask them all of this, Barringer sat in the corner, fuming. Waiting. Watching.

* * *

"Aw, I thought I was going to see Junior," Calista said to Garrison.

"Seriously?" Garrison chuckled. "You thought I was going to bring my son into a bar?"

Calista laughed. "No. I just—" Her face reddened.

"I'm teasing you," Garrison told her.

"I know. I just missed him today. It feels so weird when he's not there. I've been taking care of him since he was a tiny, little thing. I feel like he's a part of me. And he's growing so fast."

"Yeah, you know us Blackstone men grow like lumber jacks." Garrison grinned.

Calista laughed. "No kidding."

The waitress brought Garrison a beer, the one he'd requested from the bar before he sat down.

Calista took a sip of wine and studied Garrison for a moment while he glanced around the place. "Is Junior spending the night with your mom, or—?"

He caught her eyes when he said, "No. I'm

going to pick him up when I leave here. Thanks for agreeing to meet up with me. I know this is probably awkward for you."

"It's fine," she said, but this would've been a good outing for you to have with Bryson, Everson or Barry. I'm not really a bar chick."

"I thought about asking them, but I feel like I can tell you things my brothers won't quite understand, you know."

Calista nodded before taking another sip of wine.

"Who knew something like this would bring us close again?" Garrison said.

Calista cracked a half smile. "Yeah. Who knew?"

They held gazes for a moment, then Calista cleared her throat and said, "Look, Garrison. I know it was a long time ago, but if I hurt you back then—"

"Not *if*, Calista. You *did* hurt me."

"Then I'm truly sorry."

He nodded. "I know. It took me a while, but I got over it...fell in love with Vivienne. She was something else, you know. She was older than me."

"She wasn't older than you, was she?"

"Yep, by four years. Older and wiser."

"Well, let's keep it real. Women are wiser, period, no matter what their age."

Garrison chuckled. "Not necessarily." He took a sip of his beer. "It's hard being alone sometimes."

Calista nodded.

"When it's quiet in the house, I think I hear

her voice. You get used to someone being there and when they're gone, it disrupts your whole life."

"Exactly."

"Today, I found more of her things. Some perfume. Old anniversary cards I gave her. She never threw those things away. Women are sentimental that way."

"Yes we are, especially when we're in love."

"So you still have old anniversary cards and things from Barry?"

"I do. I have a lot of gifts from Barry that I cherish, but—" Calista hesitated to say the rest.

"But?"

She smiled uncomfortably. "Nothing."

"No, tell me. We're sharing. Share." He cracked a smile.

"I was going to say I have a lot of things from Barry, but I don't have..." Her eyes teared up, but she blinked them away. "I don't have Barry."

"There's no crying allowed in a bar, Cali. Only drinking."

Calista smiled, pinching tears away at the same time. "Well, in that case..." She picked up her glass and took another sip of wine. "Is that why you requested to meet me at a bar? The *no crying* rule?"

"Partially. And I really wanted a beer."

Calista cracked a smile. "You could've went by Bryson's and had a beer in his famous man cave."

Garrison grinned. "Yeah, but I don't want to talk his ears off with my problems."

"Oh, but it's okay to talk mine off."

A smile grew on his face.

"I'm teasing."

"Yes, I'm going to talk your ears off. You know what I'm going through."

"Not completely."

"You know what it's like to lose someone you love."

"A different kind of loss, but yes, I suppose you're right."

Garrison nodded.

"Hey, Garrison."

"Yes?" he said, attentively.

"Why did you tell Vivienne about us?"

"Because I felt like I needed to. She wanted you to be Junior's caretaker. She knew how much you wanted a baby. She didn't know everything we now know about Barry, but she knew you wanted a baby, so she asked me if I thought you would accept. That's when I told her. Had to."

Calista nodded.

"And I've been thinking we should also tell Barry. We shouldn't have this secret between us anymore."

"I don't think that's a good idea."

"Why not?"

"Because he's going to hit the roof when he finds out."

Garrison shrugged. "My brother needs to work on his anger issues. He knows that. I've spoken with him about it several times."

"But it's worse now. Since he told me about, you know, his *issues*, he's been resentful."

"And it doesn't help that the company is having problems," Garrison added.

"Exactly."

"Then here's what I propose we do. You're coming to the family dinner tomorrow night, right?"

"Yes. I'll be there," Calista said.

"Good. At some point, we'll pull Barry off to the side and talk to him together. Maybe if we double-team him, he'll listen."

Calista smirked. "Or maybe not."

"It's a chance we have to take, Calista. You're practically Junior's mother now."

"Don't say that, Gary."

"I am going to say it. It's true."

"So what's going to happen when you remarry?"

"I'm not going to remarry."

Calista frowned. "But—" She stopped talking when she realized how sensitive the topic was. Vivienne had only been gone for a little over three months now.

"You know what I find strange about going through this and being a widower?" Garrison asked her.

"What's that?"

"When people talk to me, they have to change their demeanor and the inflection in their voices to a softer, sadder one to express their condolences. They see me laughing, they wonder how I'm able to smile. Most people think I should be depressed all the time and yelling *why me* into the sky or something. I don't get that. I grieve all the time. My heart hurts right now, even while I'm sitting here talking to you. It hurts, but I cope. I have to, right? For my son. For my family."

"Yes. That's right. And who cares what people say, anyway?" Calista asked, remembering what Kalina told her. "It's not like they have to walk in your shoes."

Garrison turned up his beer bottle, taking long gulps. He set the empty bottle on the table and said, "Okay, so tomorrow, we'll tag team your stubborn husband."

"Hey, he's your *stubborn* brother. You've known him longer than I have."

"Which is why I know he loves you, little lady. He can't concentrate without you. I can see it as clear as day. We all can, except for him. Let's hope we make some progress tomorrow."

"We'll see."

Chapter 29

Barringer couldn't sleep a minute last night. Not even a second. He stayed up drinking. Seething. The possibility of another man, a better man, taking Calista away from him had crossed his mind before. Little did he know that man could've been his own brother. Now he was sitting at the dinner table with flaring nostrils, stewing over the possibility. Was Calista seeing Garrison?

He didn't want to go to this family dinner, but decided to go just to observe Calista and Garrison – to see if anything was going on between them. They had drinks together last night. He saw it with his own eyes, but it didn't mean they were together. Tonight, he'd find out for sure.

The family had all gathered around the dinner table. June decorated the table with tall, white candles running along the center on top of a laced table runner. The women were busy bringing out food – all cooked by June and Everson.

Barringer looked at his parents. With the turmoil in his marriage, he wondered how they'd managed to stay together and happy for so long. They made marriage look easy when it was anything but.

He glanced at Everson. Even at dinner he was on his phone. He stayed working just as much as he did. He wondered if June had a problem with Everson's work schedule, the same way Calista had an issue with his.

He looked at Candice. She was checking her watch like she couldn't wait for dinner to be over before it had a chance to start. He wondered if her impatience had anything to do with Kurt Hempstead. She was in for a rude awakening if she thought she would sneak around to see some big shot competitor behind the backs of her brothers and not get the third degree.

Bryson looked especially happy. He deserved happiness after what he'd been through. And even though he was going through his own difficulty, Barringer found a little joy knowing Bryson was happy.

After he'd given everyone a glance, he focused his attention back to Calista. She had just brought a basket of rolls to the table. Didn't even look at him when she did so. Surprisingly, she had spoken when he'd first arrived, but now, she made (and kept) herself busy to avoid him.

Garrison had yet to arrive. He wondered if

he would show.

Everyone settled around the table to their respective seats.

"Dinner looks good, young lady," Daddy Blackstone said as he rubbed his hands together, looking at June.

"I can't take all the credit. My wonderful, super talented husband helped me with everything," June said looking at Everson. He was busy on his phone again.

"Everson, put the phone down, man," Bryson said. "Your wife just gave you a compliment."

Everson looked up briefly and said, "Thanks, babe," without having any idea what June had said.

Calista unintentionally caught Barringer's gaze, quickly looking away. The last time she and Barringer hosted a family dinner, she remembered arguing with him. Boy had she been tempted to throw a piece of steak at his thick, hard head, but what was the point. A person wouldn't change unless they were ready to make a change, and the only thing Barringer Blackstone was ready for was an opportunity to make a dollar.

"Does anyone know if Garrison is coming?" Elowyn asked.

Everson shrugged.

June scrunched up her face. "You think he's up to it?"

Calista discreetly checked her phone, but she wasn't discreet enough because Barringer knew exactly what she was doing. She slid her phone back into her purse and said, "He'll be here. Probably running a little behind trying to get Junior together and all."

"I don't want to sound rude, but should we start eating?" Candice asked.

And all eyes were on her...

"What?" she asked with a smirk on her face. "A sister is hungry."

"A sister seems like she's in a hurry for some reason," Bryson said.

Barringer grinned.

Bryson watched Candice like a hawk. She thought since he was preoccupied with Kalina, she'd be free of his overprotective ways, but he still made time to keep tabs on her. He knew all about her little run-in with Kurt Hempstead.

At the sound of the doorbell, Everson stood and said, "That's probably Gary right there." He walked swiftly to the door. "Hey, you made it, man. We were just talking about you and Junior."

Calista smiled, thrilled Garrison decided to join them after all. When he walked into the dining room, all the women, except for her, got up to hug him, even Elowyn.

"So glad you made it, son," Elowyn said, "And look at my baby." She wasted no time taking Junior from his car seat.

"Good to see you, Garrison," Kalina told him.

"Looking good, bro," June said.

"Hey, Gary," Candice said. "Mom, don't hog the baby. We need to pass him around the table like a dish so everybody can get a kiss from those cheeks."

Kalina laughed. "He looks like a dish, don't he? Like a glass casserole of buttery candied yams with marshmallows."

"Mmm...did you make yams?" Candice asked.

Bryson squinted at Candice. She was especially happy tonight for some reason.

"You made it," Calista said, evenly, when she saw Garrison making his way around the table to where she was sitting. He leaned down and hugged her, then whispered in her ear, "So far, so good, right?"

Calista nodded.

Barringer frowned. What was all the whispering about?

Garrison took a seat next to Barringer, patting him on the shoulder as he sat down. "Hey, Barry."

"Hey," Barringer said, but it came across so dry, he may as well had kept his mouth shut.

Garrison scanned the dishes on the table and said, "Everson, you and June cooked up a feast, I see."

"Yeah. We wanted a good, hearty meal for the people we love," Everson said.

"Aw," Candice drawled out. "Now let's eat."

"How about letting pops pray first, Candy?" Bryson said.

Theodore stood up, prayed over the meal. Afterwards, everyone took the dish closest to them, and passed clockwise around the table.

Junior made some cooing noises.

Calista leaned forward to get a better view of

him. She missed him yesterday and seeing him now brought a smile to her face. Garrison had dressed him in a pair of navy blue jeans and a shirt she'd bought him that read: *If you think I'm handsome, you should see my daddy.*

"My grandbaby is trying to talk already," Elowyn said. "Look at you, handsome. Grandma likes your shirt."

Everyone turned to look at Junior's T-shirt onesie.

"Oh, I know Garrison picked that out," Candice said. She looked at him and whispered, "So vain."

"Actually, Calista bought him that shirt," Garrison said.

"Guilty," Calista said. "It was so cute, I couldn't resist." She could feel the heat of Barringer's eyes from across the table which is why she avoided making eye contact with him.

Barringer took a sip of water, hoping the ice in the glass would help to calm the burning anger he felt shooting through his veins. A sip turned into finishing the glass, and it still hadn't provided any relief.

"Look at the way he responds to your voice," Elowyn said to Calista. "Look at him. He's looking right at you."

Calista smiled. Seeing baby Junior look at her with longing eyes warmed her heart. Then he began squirming. Crying.

"Aw...he wants you, Cali."

Bad idea. Calista knew that. "Um, just give him the bottle. He should be okay."

"No, no, no, honey. He wants you," Elowyn

said. "Come on over here and get him."

Calista tried not to frown. She didn't want to hold Junior right now, not while Barringer was here.

"I got him," Kalina said, taking Junior from Elowyn's grasp. She winked at Calista. "Okay, lil' man. What is it that you want? Hunh? Why are you giving Auntie Kalina a hard time?" Kalina was able to settle him enough so he'd take his bottle.

Calista instantly felt a wave of relief after such a close call.

Dishes had ceased being passed and everyone was eating now, everyone except for Barringer, that is, Calista noticed.

"So, Gary, did Barry talk to you about the future of BFSG?" Theodore asked.

"No," Garrison said. He glanced over at Barringer. "I've been out of the loop on that."

"I don't want to put you on the spot, but how have you been doing, Gary?" Candice asked, "You know after—"

"We don't have to talk about that right at the moment," Bryson said, interrupting her.

"No, it's fine, Bryce," Garrison said. He looked at Candice. "I'm getting by...taking it one day at a time and, ah—" Garrison stopped talking to look at Calista. He remembered her advice, deciding to give Candice and the rest of the family an honest answer. "I don't know how I'm making it. I miss Vivienne. Every day I miss her, and it's not getting any easier with the passing of time. If anything, it's becoming more and more difficult. But I'm—" Garrison stopped talking to even his breaths and control his emotions. "I'm trying."

"We all miss her," Elowyn said. "She left a vacancy in our little family."

Theodore nodded. "She certainly did."

Calista glanced up at Barringer, watching his direct gaze back at her. He still hadn't touched his food. She turned her attention to Garrison to see how he was holding up. He looked flushed, but had managed to keep it together enough to take a few bites of his meal. She smiled. He'd conquered his fear of talking to the family about Vivienne.

Junior contorted his body, beginning to unravel again in Kalina's lap.

"Oh, you're a wiggly little thing, aren't you?" Kalina said, holding him close. She set his bottle on the table.

"Did he burp yet?" Calista asked, watching little Junior look at her as she did so.

"I don't know," Kalina said.

"Try to give him the pacifier," Calista told her.

Now, Junior had let out a full cry. A loud, mean one.

Struggling, Kalina asked, "Where is the pacifier?"

"On the right side of the diaper bag," Calista and Garrison said together. In unison. The exact same words.

Kalina dug around in the bag, found the pacifier but when she popped it in his mouth, he spit it right back out, his cries filling the dining room. "He doesn't want it."

Garrison stood up, took a few steps towards Kalina and said, "Come on, lil' man," taking his son in his arms. "He was a little fussy last night, too. Was he like this yesterday, mother?"

"A little. Then he ate and went to sleep."

Garrison held Junior against his shoulder and said, "It's okay, lil' man," but Junior kept on crying.

"Maybe he's sleepy," Candice said.

"No, he's not sleepy," Garrison told her. "He slept before we got here."

Calista looked at Garrison as he tried to calm Junior down. Everything inside of her ached to hold the baby. She'd been taking care of him since birth. She had an attachment to him. They'd bonded. Junior was practically her son. But she didn't want to hold the baby now, not here in front of Barringer. He was already stressed. She knew that. She didn't want to add to his frustration. But she didn't want to hear Junior cry either.

"Here," June said, walking around the table to take Junior. "Come to Auntie June."

Junior cried even more when June took him.

Garrison knew who Junior wanted. Kalina knew who the baby wanted. He wanted Calista. His...his mother.

June returned to her seat, next to Calista, and said, "Shh...stop all that fuss lil' Garrison. Everything is okay. You just want one of those chicken legs, don't you?"

Everyone laughed.

"But you can't have one," June continued. "You don't have any teeth yet, baby."

Junior didn't find anything funny. He was steadily crying until Calista's heart couldn't take it anymore. "Here, I'll take him, June."

"Okay," June said handing him to Calista.

Calista cradled Junior in her arms and his cries instantly stopped. "There. It's okay, sweet boy." She automatically kissed his cheek.

Garrison smiled, then resumed eating.

Candice glanced up at Barringer, feeling sorry for her brother. She saw the veins at his temples swell. Saw his jaw clench. Face flush. *This is not good*, she thought. She tried to tell Calista it wasn't a good idea for Barringer to see her with Junior, but apparently, Calista didn't get the point. Or maybe she did and just didn't care. Did she resent Barringer *that* much?

"See. That's all he wanted," Elowyn said. "He's really taken to you, Calista."

Calista smiled uncomfortably. She dared to look up at Barringer.

Now that Junior was calm and quiet, forks clanking against plates could be heard, along with smooth jazz playing from the living room.

Barringer still hadn't touched his food. He sat back in his chair, looking at Calista holding Garrison's baby and something broke inside of him because it was then he realized he would never be able to give her a baby. And she was good with Junior. She held him like she was a mother already. Like she'd had practice. Some women were naturals at motherhood. She was one of those women.

Barringer stood up.

"Barry, where are you going?" Candice

asked.

"I just remembered...I have somewhere to be. Enjoy dinner, guys," he responded.

"Oh, come on, Barringer," Elowyn said. "Don't ruin this for us."

"Mother—"

"We're finally able to all be here as a family and you're leaving," she finished saying. "Please stay, son."

"I can't," he said. He took a final glance at Calista holding Junior. "I can't. I'm going to go."

Elowyn shook her head, was almost near tears when she heard the door close behind him.

Everyone took turns sneaking glances at Calista.

Attempting to smooth things over, Candice said, "It's all right, Mom. Barringer will be fine. I'll check on him later." She sounded calm, but really she could scream. How could Calista do this?

Chapter 30

Instead of driving home, Barringer drove to Garrison's house, parked out front and waited. He decided it would be best to confront him this way, in private, instead of in front of the family. He'd been torturing himself, holding his anger in for so long, he had to get up and walk away from the dinner table tonight. Otherwise, the vision he had of repeatedly punching Garrison in the face would've become reality then and there.

Then there was the matter of seeing Calista holding Garrison's baby. That simple act intensified his anger. Made him bitter. Jealous. What was so wrong with him that he couldn't give Calista a baby? Was this some kind of punishment? He didn't know at the moment. What he *did* know is, he would find out why Garrison was having drinks with Calista last night.

* * *

He'd waited two hours and now, Garrison was pulling up in the driveway. Garrison parked, took Junior's car seat from the back and headed for the door. He saw Barringer parked out front and figured he'd either sit there or get out sooner or later. For now, he had to get his son inside.

Barringer jumped out of the car. He quietly headed in the direction of his brother. He honestly didn't know what he would do. He was tired. Angry. No, furious. After watching Calista laugh it up with Garrison – those images in his head all day had done a number on him.

"Is there something you needed, Barry?" Garrison asked, unlocking the door with his right hand while holding the car seat with his left. The diaper bag was swinging from his left shoulder.

"Yeah. There's something I need to ask you."

Garrison walked inside.

Barringer was steps behind him.

"Okay, um...let me put Junior in his crib. I'll be right back."

Barringer used the time to look around the living room. He hadn't been to Garrison's house in quite some time. He noticed Garrison had taken down all the pictures of Vivienne from the walls.

Nearing the bottom of the stairs, Garrison said, "If this is work-related, don't bother."

Barringer glanced up at his brother. "Has

nothing to do with work, Gary."

"Well, what is it?" Garrison asked, walking to stand near him.

Barringer frowned. There was no easy way to ask it, so he decided to come right out with it. "Are you sleeping with my wife?"

"What?" Garrison frowned.

"I'm not asking it twice."

"What kind of question is that, Barry?"

"One I need you to answer," he scowled.

Garrison glared at his brother. "I'm not going to justify your ridiculous question with answer."

"Then how about this one? Why were you at a bar, sharing drinks with my wife last night? Can you answer that one?"

"Sure. I'll answer it. I told her I needed to talk. She agreed to meet me there."

Now, the brothers were standing a few feet apart glaring at each other.

Garrison tried to keep a cool head because he knew his brother usually kept a hot one. "Listen, Barry, I don't know what your intention was in coming here, but—"

"I want to know if you're sleeping with my wife, Gary," Barringer asked, eyes burning with rage. He shoved Garrison, twice, while asking the question again.

Garrison caught his balance. "You need to calm down, Barry. I'm not going to fight you."

"You're sleeping with my wife?" Barringer shoved him again.

Garrison balanced himself then rubbed the nape of his neck. As calmly as he could muster, he said, "No. Calista has been taking care of Junior. Vivienne personally asked her to do so before she died. There. She's taking care of my son. Does that answer your question?"

"Right. She's taking care of *your* son. *Your* son, huh? Was that a shot at me?" Barringer asked with flaring nostrils.

"I'm not taking shots at you, Barry. Jeez, man."

"Yeah. Spending your time with my wife is more of your speed."

"Man, I just told you—"

"Then why are you two so close all of a sudden? Hunh?"

Garrison sighed, rubbed his head and said, "There's nothing all-of-a-sudden about me and Calista's relationship. I should've told you this before, Barry. I had planned on telling you tonight, but you left dinner early. So here goes...I've known Calista since before you two were married."

Barringer looked at his brother with a dark, heated gaze that could cut through steel. "Come again?"

"We used to date. In college."

Barringer's breaths became rapid. Chest heavy. He took a few, small, predatory steps closer to his brother. "I don't think I heard you correctly."

"Barry, you need to calm down, man."

"What do you mean you *used* to date her?"

"In college, before she even knew you existed, we dated."

Barringer shoved his brother again to the

point where Garrison almost fell, but he caught himself.

Garrison brushed it off. "Barry—"

"You dated *my* Calista?"

"Like I said, it was before she knew you."

"So you slept with her?" Barringer asked with criminal eyes.

"Barry—"

"Did you sleep with her?" he asked again, but already knew the answer to the question before the words left his mouth.

"That was in the past. Again, we were in college. We were dating. We're not dating now. She's your wife and no, I'm not sleeping with your wife, Barry. We spend time together because she helps me with Junior and I can talk to her, and quite frankly, I appreciate her being there for me."

"Wow. Unbelievable."

Garrison took a breath. "I lost my wife. Vivienne is gone. Calista, Kalina, Candice, June, Everson and Bryson...they were there for me. Where were you, Barry? Where were you? When I'm here alone trying to figure out how I'm going to make it from one day to the next, where are you?"

Barringer frowned.

"This is the first time you've been over here since Vivienne passed. Do you realize that? First time. And it's not to see how I'm coping. It's to confront me because you think Calista and I are sleeping together. Newsflash, Barry. Selfish people and marriage don't mix. That's why your marriage has fallen apart. Has nothing to do with me. It's you. You're selfish. You lied to Calista. Presented yourself as someone you were not. Now, you have to live with that decision."

Barringer stood motionless as he glared at his brother.

Garrison continued, "If you want to blame someone for your failed marriage, look in the mirror, man. I'm no threat to your marriage. Calista has been an anchor for me, and I'm grateful to her for taking care of Junior, because I can't do it on my own."

Barringer turned around, left Garrison standing in the living room as he headed for the front door. He started his car, slammed on the gas and with tires squealing he headed for his next destination – Calista's apartment.

Chapter 31

Thoughts another human being should never have about another ran through Barringer's mind as he raced to Calista's place. He'd nearly lost control of the Porsche several times, but that didn't signal him to slow down. He drove like he felt – like an out-of-control maniac. Out of his mind. He had no idea what he would do once he arrived. Once he laid eyes on her.

She moved out of their home – wanted to start a new life and gave him the third degree because he kept a secret from her when she'd been keeping one from him – she used to date his brother. Why hadn't she told him *that* before they married? Was she afraid he wouldn't want to marry her if he found out, and if so, wouldn't that put them both in the wrong? Did they not do the exact same thing? Keep a secret from each other for the sake of the relationship?

He swiftly emerged from the car and rang the doorbell, repeatedly. More times than he could count. He pushed and pushed and pushed. If she was sleeping, too bad. She was going to answer this door. Tonight.

Calista sat up in bed, glancing at the clock. Who'd lost their mind and was ringing her doorbell frantically so close to midnight? Then a thought hit her. Maybe it was Garrison. What if something was wrong with Junior?

She jumped out of bed, walked quickly to the door. When she peered through the peephole, she was surprised to see Barringer standing there. He looked angry. Out of himself. His look scared her so much, she didn't know whether or not to open the door. So instead, she said loud enough for him to hear, "What is it, Barringer?"

"Open the door," he said, his voice forced, eyes filled with anger.

"Why?"

"Because I asked you to open the door. I need to talk to you. Now."

Without responding, she turned the deadbolt lock.

Barringer took it from there. He pushed the door open and invited himself in.

"What is it, Barry?"

"You tried to make me feel bad for what I did to you, but you're no better than me. No better."

"What are you talking about?" she asked, frowning. His back was to her. She'd just closed the front door.

Barringer turned around to face her. "I'm talking about the fact that you and Garrison had a *thing*, and I didn't know any*thing* about it. No wonder you're so close. Rekindling old times, huh?"

"You have the wrong idea."

"No, I have it right."

"Barry—"

He held up his hand. "Did you or did you not have a relationship with my brother?"

Calista sighed heavily. Garrison must've told him.

"Silence. Yeah, that's what I thought," Barringer said. "You—" he shook his head. "You were in a relationship with my brother and you kept it from me, just like I knew I couldn't have children and I kept that from you."

"It's not the same, Barry."

"It is the same!" he roared, walking up to her crowding her personal space. "But it's all good, Calista. You and Garrison can run off into the sunset for all I care and live happily ever after."

"Barry—"

"You wanted a baby. You got one. You wanted a better man. You got one. Have a nice, happy life, Calista."

"Barry, will you—"

"Don't say another word to me, girl, because I don't even know what I'm capable of at the moment," he said through gritted teeth.

Calista's eyes filled with tears as she watched him snatch the front door open.

Before walking through it, Barringer turned to her again. "I saw you with him at the bar last night. Saw how happy you were. How happy he made you. How your face glowed when you two laughed and joked...I don't know what you were talking about, but you were happy. And I sat there and watched my wife enjoy the company of another man, my brother, while all kinds of sinister thoughts ran through my mind. Thoughts a man should never have about his wife or his brother."

He stared at her for a moment, finding it difficult to breathe with the pounding in his ears and the adrenaline rushing throughout his body. "You left me," he finally said. "Left us in limbo. Well, I'll do us both a favor. We're not in limbo anymore because *I'm* telling *you* it's over."

Tears fell from her eyes. "Barry—"

"Don't talk to me."

"Barry, please just—"

"I said, don't talk to me!" he yelled, veins swelling in his neck. Temples throbbing so wildly, he felt lightheaded. "I'll pack up all your stuff and leave it in the foyer, or on the curb...whichever's more convenient for you. Goodbye, Calista." He slammed the door when he exited, so hard that Calista jumped.

She walked over to the couch, sat there and cried because it was official. Their marriage was over, confirmed by a slamming door.

Chapter 32

Two Weeks Later

Barringer woke up on the brown leather couch in the family room. His clothes reeked of beer. So did the room. Empty beer bottles littered the table, along with old takeout containers. He hadn't been to work in two weeks. He told Candice he was taking a short vacation. Only thing was, he didn't tell her when he'd be coming back. How could he tell her when he didn't know himself? There was no use in going to work when he couldn't work. Besides, staying at home and drinking one's self to oblivion was a lot easier than trying to save a multi-million dollar company. Doing nothing required no effort. So he stayed home and drank, laid around and did nothing. Crazy how when Calista was there, he was gone all the time. Now she was gone and he was there.

The house was a mess. Calista was the one

who cleaned and spruced up the place. And sometimes, she'd arrange for the cleaning agency to come by for deep cleanings. Barringer had no idea what service she used. He could probably find out if he made an effort.

He sighed, stared up at the ceiling and thought about Calista. He told her, two weeks ago he'd pack her things and leave them in the foyer, but he hadn't touched anything she owned. He shut himself off from the outside world and only answered the door for food deliveries. No one else.

He didn't answer when Bryson stopped by with Everson. He didn't answer the door for his father, nor did he answer his phone for his mother, Candice or Kalina. He wanted to be left alone. The family eventually got the hint.

That's why the knocks at the front door irritated him. Feeling like his head was about to explode from the loud bangs, he rushed to the door to see which one of his brothers he was going to have to punch in the face. When he snatched the door open, his expression softened when he saw his sister standing there instead. He looked at her hand. When did she grow an iron fist?

"Goodness, Barry. You look like crap," Candice said.

Dismissing her critique, he asked, "Do you realize how loud you were knocking?"

"Actually, that was me," Bryson said, standing to the right of Candice, initially out of sight of Barringer, but came into view now, presenting himself.

Barringer scrubbed a hand down his unshaven face. "You should've taken my not answering the phone as a hint that I wanted to be left alone."

"Nah, caveman. We've had enough of leaving you alone," Bryson said, inviting himself in.

Candice followed.

Barringer dispelled a breath. "Whatever you two have up your sleeves, I'm not in the mood."

"We just want to talk," Candice said. "Wanted to see how you were doing."

"I'm fine, now can you—?"

"How long are you going to do this, Barry?" Bryson asked.

Barringer raised a brow. "Do what?"

"This," Bryson said gesturing with his palms out. "You're sulking, preferring misery over the life you could have."

"Sound familiar?" Barringer shot back.

"How many times are you going to bring up my situation with Felicia?"

"I'm bringing it up because you were somewhat of a recluse after it all went down. Now you're judging me."

"I'm not judging you, Barry. I'm trying to help you. Felicia cheated on me and decided to leave. Calista wouldn't do that to you."

Barringer sneered. "She and Garrison have gotten pretty comfortable. And two weeks ago, Garrison told me he used to date Calista in college...guess since his wife died, he wants to take mine."

Bryson shook his head at Barringer's heartless comment.

Candice frowned. "Gary wouldn't do that. So what, they dated in college. That was college. This isn't about them dating in college, is it? It's about seeing Calista with Junior."

Barringer narrowed his eyes at his sister. "Why aren't you at work?"

"Because it's Saturday. You've lost track of your days, too?"

Barringer walked near the breakfast nook, staring out into the sunny backyard.

"Listen, Barry. I know how it is to lose someone you love. When I lost Felicia, I swore up and down that I would never get married again. I was depressed...wanted to be alone. I couldn't sleep in my own bedroom because I used to share it with her. Everywhere I turned, something in my house reminded me of her. Remember when I wanted to sell the house because I didn't want those memories?"

Barringer nodded.

"It threw my life off course, which is what Calista has done to you. Your life is off course, and you're not sure if you can get it back on track. You're worried that if you try and things don't work out, you're a failure, so doing nothing seems like the right thing at the moment. But you can't afford to sit around and do nothing. You have a company in limbo while you decide what to do with your personal life. People are depending on you and let's face it. You're not going to find another woman to put up with your crap like Calista. I'm going to keep it real with you for a minute, man. You're kind of a jerk, Barry."

"Yeah. Colton to the tenth power," Candice said, then giggled.

"Well, not *that* bad," Bryson said.

Turning to look at his brother and sister with his arms crossed, Barringer said, "You make a good point, Bryce, but I don't know how our marriage will ever be the same again given the fact that I can't give Calista what she wants."

"You can. There's always adoption. You and Calista will be ideal parents to some beautiful children who need a home. She's already good with Junior. You saw the way she handled him at dinner."

Barringer nodded. "Yeah. She would've been a good mother."

"And still will be," Candice said.

"Talk to her," Bryson said. "Do it today. Not tomorrow. You see how weeks have quickly turned into four months. Four months, Calista has been gone. Now, in the words of Theodore Blackstone, I'm putting my foot down."

Barringer grinned.

Candice smiled. "You know when daddy puts his foot down, he means business."

"As do I," Bryson said.

"Well, look, man...I have to go. Kalina is waiting for me. We're heading to Hilton Head for a few days."

"Great." Candice said. "You're going to Hilton Head and I'm doing laundry. Can't wait until my dream guy sweeps me off my feet."

Barringer and Bryson both frowned at her.

"What?" she asked. "Y'all act like I can't

date."

"You can't," the brothers responded together.

Candice shook her head.

Bryson threw an arm around Barringer. "If you need to talk, just call."

Candice walked over to him, enveloped him in a hug. "I love you, care bear."

"Love you too, sis," he said. "Now get out of here. Scat."

Candice grinned. "You're kicking me out now?"

"He's putting us both out," Bryson said.

* * *

After he shaved and showered, Barringer left the house for a trip to the barber. From there, the headed to Garrison's house. He had no idea if his brother would be home. He just knew he needed to talk to him.

He pulled up in the driveway. Garrison's car was there, so he walked up to the door, rang the bell and was surprised at how quickly Garrison opened it.

"I saw you pull up, so I figured I'd meet you at the door," Garrison said. "What's up?"

Barringer grimaced. "Do you have a minute?"

"Sure. Come in."

Barringer slid his hands in the front pockets of his jeans and said, "I came here to talk to you about the last time I was here. I was out of mind—"

"Barry," Garrison said, cutting him off. "It's water under the bridge, man."

"No, let me say this. I wasn't there for you when you lost Vivienne. I had my own problems, and I was selfishly dealing with that."

Garrison nodded. "And you need to know I'm not, in any way, involved with Calista. She's like a sister to me, Barry, and Vivienne had specifically requested Calista take care of Garrison, Junior. She wanted her to be his caretaker because she knew how badly Calista wanted a child, and she was certain Calista would be good with him."

Barringer nodded.

"If you're not okay with it—"

"I'm not going to lie, Gary. It bothered me to see her with Junior. Now, I understand. I get it. I'm sorry I let jealousy and anger get in the way of getting to know my own nephew. My only nephew. Where is he, by the way?"

Garrison grinned. "Funny you should ask. He's with Calista. He's usually with me on Saturdays since she keeps him through the weekdays, but today, she wanted to take him to some exhibit at the children's museum."

Barringer smirked. "She would've been a good mother."

"She *is* a good mother. She's Garrison, Junior's mother. And don't worry too much about not having a child. I hope it happens for you and Calista one day, but even if it doesn't, my son is your son, too. We're brothers, Barry. We have to navigate through this life together.

We're both going through trying times right now, but it'll get better."

Barringer walked over to his brother and clasped his hand, throwing his other arm around his back and patting him there. "Thanks, Garrison. I owe you."

"Good. Then you can give me my job back."

Barringer smirked. "I'm surprised you want it back."

"I didn't at first, but Calista told me you needed help."

Eyebrows raised, he asked, "Calista told you I needed help?"

"Yep."

"How would she know?"

Garrison shrugged. "She's *your* wife. Who knows you better than she does?"

Barringer grinned. "I suppose you're right."

"So what's this I hear about a possible merger with The Champion Corporation?"

Barringer shook his head. "Pops thinks it's a good idea. Says it'll ensure job security. We'll discuss it first thing Monday morning."

"Does that mean I have the job?"

"Gary, you always had the job. Why do you think I never filled the position?"

Garrison's mouth lifted into a lopsided grin. "Thanks, Barry."

"You won't be thanking me when you realize how much work you have to do."

"I'm sure I'll manage," he said. Calista was right. Work would help him take his mind off of Vivienne. Off of everything that wasn't right in his life. He was up for the challenge.

Chapter 33

After dropping off Junior, Calista went straight home and took a shower. Now, she was standing in the kitchen, making a pot of chili – a big pot like she was having company, but no one was coming over. Usually, when she made chili (when she was still living at home), she'd invite the family over for a bowl and everyone had their own special way of eating it. She remembered how Vivienne used to like hers layered in sweet onions. Bryson preferred sour cream. June and Everson used crackers, not spoons, to eat their chili. Candice would sprinkle cheese in her bowl then pour chili on top of it. And Barringer would pour chili in a bowl, mix in a handful of oyster crackers, then top it off with sour cream, cheddar cheese and green onions. She smiled. She remembered calling him odd. He said it was genius.

She missed him.

At the museum today with Junior, she saw

many families, couples with their children, looking around and spending quality time together. That made her think of Barringer. She missed him, and not just the four months they'd been separated. She missed talking to him and interacting with him for years.

Her ringing cell phone took her out of a reminiscent mood. She saw Candice's name on the display.

"Hey, Candy."

"Hey, Calista. What you up to?"

"I'm making chili."

"Chili?"

"Yes. Why did you say that like a question? Like I'm not supposed to be making chili?" Calista laughed.

"I'm just wondering where my invite went."

Calista grinned. "I didn't invite anyone. It's just me."

"You want some company? I can call up June. Kalina's out of town."

Calista chewed her lip. She could use some company, but she didn't want the girls to think she needed them to stop whatever they were doing just to be by her side. She wasn't bored. Okay, she was a little bored, but it wasn't nothing TV couldn't fix. So she responded, "That's okay, Candy. I'm fine."

"Oh, come on, Cali. I can pick up June on the way. Everson's not home, so you know she's bored."

"All right."

"Yes!" Candice said. "I'll call her right now."

"Okay. See you soon."

Calista smiled. It wouldn't be a drab Saturday evening after all.

Her phone rang again before she could stir the chili. Had Candice gotten a confirmation from June in mere seconds?

She looked at the phone and saw Garrison's name on the display. She answered quickly. "Everything okay?" Then she realized something was wrong. She could hear Junior crying.

"Not really...can't find his pacifier."

"I clamped it to his onesie."

"Well, it has officially grown legs."

"Oh, no," Calista said.

"Can you check your back seat to make sure it didn't fall off in the car?"

"Okay, sure. Hold on...I need to get some shoes."

"Thanks, Calista. I'm sorry about this. I know this is your rest time, especially after you've had him for most of the day."

"It's okay," Calista said, stepping into her shoes. "I wasn't sleeping. I'm in here cooking."

"Cooking?"

Calista smiled. "Yes. Cooking."

"What are you making?"

Calista opened the door, pulled it closed, then walked straight for her car. "Chili."

"You're making chili?"

She grinned. "Yes. I'm making chili."

"Ain't that something? You're making chili and a brother can't get an invite."

Calista laughed while opening the car door. She saw Junior's pacifier lying on the back seat.

"Got it...just found Junior's pacifier in my back seat. That little rebel snatched it off. He's pretty strong to be four months old."

"Gets it from his daddy."

Calista grinned.

"All right. So it's settled," Garrison said. "Now that I have an excuse to come over there, you're going to have me some chili ready to go, right?"

Smiling, Calista said, "Sure, Gary. It'll be ready."

'Then I'll see you in a few."

* * *

Garrison had come and gone, retrieving a big Tupperware bowl of chili and Junior's pacifier. Amazing how babies liked one particular pacifier and wouldn't touch the others. She knew Garrison had a collection of pacifiers. It was a baby shower favorite. But Junior wanted that particular one. The soft, gummy green one.

June and Candice sat in the living room watching TV while eating their chili. Every other minute or so, they exclaimed how good it was.

Calista stayed in the kitchen, debating on whether or not she should set some aside for Barringer. She wondered how he would react if she brought some over to his house. He had been in rare form lately, and the last time he stormed into her apartment, she felt threatened. She'd never felt that way with him before.

"Cali, bring your bowl and come sit down with us," Candice said.

"Okay," Calista said, snapping out of her reverie. "Be right there, ladies."

She left the chili simmering on low in case anyone wanted seconds. Then, with her bowl of chili and a side of crackers, she sat on the couch in between Candice and June.

"Mmm, this is what I needed in my life," June exclaimed.

Calista laughed. "It's not *that* good, June."

"Oh, yes it is."

Candice agreed, then said, "Okay, so do y'all remember the guy I was telling you about?"

"Sure. The one you claimed was bothering you at the Riverwalk, but yet, you couldn't stop smiling while telling us the story," Calista said.

"I wasn't smiling."

"Oh, yes you were," Calista said. "June back me up on this."

"You were, Candy," June chimed in. "Must've been some guy."

"Oh, whatever. Anyway, what I was going to say was, he showed up at work a few weeks ago," Candice told them.

With raised brows, June asked, "At Blackstone Financial?"

"Yep."

"He's stalking you now?" Calista asked.

"No," Candice said. "Remember I told you he gave me his business card and he worked for some company called TCC?"

"No, but continue," June said.

"Well, apparently, TCC stands for The Champion Corporation."

Kalina covered her mouth, surprised. "He works for The Champion Corporation?"

"Yes. The company that wants to bring on Blackstone Financial as a division of their company. He showed up at the office with one of the company's big wigs and presented me and Barringer with a report on why we should take the deal."

"Wow. That's ballsy," June said.

"I can see smoke coming out of Barry's ears right now," Calista said.

"Girl, Barry was heated. He got up, stormed out of the meeting and left me there."

"He left you there alone with your crush and the big wig?" June asked, mildly amused.

Unable to remove the smile from her face, Candice replied, "He's not my crush, but yes, Barry was so angry, he left me there. That's when Kurt asked me out for a drink."

"Really?" June said.

"Yeah. Really."

Pointing with a cracker, June said, "So the competition asked you out?" She crammed the cracker inside of her mouth.

"Yes he did, and that's why I didn't go, and why I didn't answer his call. Conflict of interest."

"Well, if TCC ends up being the parent company of Blackstone Financial, there will be no conflict of interest," Calista said. "Only interest."

"Not sure if that's going to happen.

Barringer didn't seem interested, but we all know Barringer isn't thinking straight these days. Ahem," Candice said, looking at Calista.

Calista smirked. "You need some water or something, Candy?"

June laughed.

"Look, Cali...when are you and Barringer getting back together?" Candice asked. "I've had enough of this nonsense."

"Not sure if we are," Calista said.

"Do you want him back?"

Calista thought for a moment. "I don't want the man I left. I want the man I married, and Barringer hasn't been that man in years."

"Then make him be that man again."

"You can't *make* a man do something he doesn't want to do," Calista said. "Men are stubborn. Some more than others, and to that end, I have the cream of the crop."

"Well, I think you're being a little stubborn, too," Candice said. "You're not making any efforts."

Calista's mouth fell open.

"Tell me one thing you've done to make things work with Barringer," Candice said.

"All those years I cooked and cleaned, only to be last place in his—"

"No, no, no, no. I'm not talking about when you two were together. I'm talking right now. What have you done to get back with him in the four months y'all have been apart?"

Calista knew the answer which is why she didn't want to say it. She hadn't done much of anything to help them get back together. "I called him once."

"Once?"

"Yes, and he was extremely impolite. Oh, and he came by here two weeks ago to confront me...it was the same night we had dinner at your place, June."

"It was pretty obvious he was a little upset that night," June said.

Calista raised her eyebrows. "A little? He basically told me to run off and live happily ever after with Garrison. He said I always wanted a baby and now I had one...he was spewing all kinds of things at me."

"I knew it. I knew something like this was going to happen," Candice said. "I tried to warn you."

"Wait," June said. "Why would Barry tell you to run off with Garrison? Did he think you two were involved or something?"

"Yeah. He did." Calista sighed. "Me and Garrison used to date in college."

June's eyes brightened. "Really?"

"Yep. Barringer didn't know until Gary told him, and I'm glad he told him because I didn't want any secrets between me and Barringer. So after he talked with Garrison, Barringer came over here to confront me and that's when he told me to ride off into the sunset with Garrison...told me to have a nice life. That we were over."

"Again, he's a hothead. You were married to him for five years and you didn't know Barry was like that?" Candice asked.

"I did, but he was also sweet. Charming.

Now, he's angry and frustrated all the time. And he has no time for me whatsoever."

"Just make an effort, Cali," Candice said. "A little effort can go a long way."

Calista sighed heavily. "I suppose you're right."

"I *am* right," Candice said, standing up, walking to the kitchen to get more chili. "You know you miss him."

"I do miss him," Calista said, feeling warmth flood through her.

"Then, make an effort. Don't even think about it. Just do it."

She nodded. "I will."

Chapter 34

When the girls left, Calista slipped into a sleepshirt and relaxed in the center of the bed with a small bowl of chocolate chip ice cream. She kept her phone nearby in case she worked up the nerve to call Barringer. She had decided against taking chili by his house especially after images of him snatching the bowl out of her hand and tossing it out into the yard flashed in her mind. It wasn't funny, but the vision made her laugh.

"What am I going to do with you, Barringer?" she said softly.

Candice told her to make an effort. But the thing about making an effort is, what if the other party wasn't willing to make any efforts? Then what?

She glanced at the clock. She wondered if Barringer was home at nine-thirty at night. He was probably at the office she concluded. He stayed working. She decided to send him a text.

Calista: Hi

He probably won't even text me back, Calista thought. He usually didn't like corresponding this way – strange considering how far technology had advanced and he kept track of it all, but he couldn't tolerate text messaging.

Barringer: Hi

Her lips quirked up. Well, what do you know? He responded.

Calista: are you home?

She nervously chewed on her bottom lip anticipating his answer.

Barringer: why are you text messaging me?

Her heart sank. Okay, so he wasn't in a good mood. She couldn't say she was surprised. She'd made an effort, and he wasn't willing to make one. Then:

Barringer: I meant, why are you texting me because you know I don't like texting.

"Oh," Calista said out loud now that she understood what he was trying to say. Still, her heart pounded in her chest, especially when she responded:

Calista: if I call, will you answer?
Barringer: only one way to find out.

"O-kay," Calista said, eyebrows raised. After a deep breath that did nothing to reduce the tension in her stomach, she said, "All right, Candy. You said make an effort. I'm making an effort."

She dialed his number, then waited. The first ring made even more knots form in her stomach. Then came ring number two. Three. He still hadn't answered. Then:

"Hi, Calista."

His deep voice ran through her entire body as she soaked it in. It was like feeling his large hands against her bare back.

"Are you there?" he asked.

"Y-yeah. Hi, Barry."

The line went quiet. She didn't know what to say. He wasn't saying anything. Since she made the call, it was on her to keep the conversation going, so she said, "Are you home?"

"Why?"

Why? Calista shook her head. Why not answer the question? "I made some chili and I know how much you like it, so I was going to bring you some."

The line went quiet again.

Calista felt her breath catch. Maybe calling him was a bad idea since he wasn't particularly in a talking mood. She couldn't decipher what kind of mood he was in.

"Barry?"

"No, I'm not home," he said.

"Oh." *Well, there goes that idea.* "Okay, well sorry to have bothered you."

"Calista."

"Yes?"

"Is that really why you called me? To bring me some chili?"

"Yes, but—"

"But what?"

Calista grinned uncomfortably. "Nothing. Never mind." Calista hung up the phone before she had a chance to embarrass herself any further. She dropped the phone on the bed and covered her face with her hands. "Ugh. I don't know why I try."

She uncovered her face when she heard her phone buzzing. She looked at the display, frowning when she saw Barringer's number. He was calling back. Why was he calling back when he seemed so irritable? So quiet. Did he not know how awkward it was for her to be on the phone when he wouldn't make an effort to have a conversation, or did he not care?

She shook her head. Instead of picking up the phone, she opted for the bowl, deciding to finish her ice cream before it melted.

Curious to see if Barringer left a voicemail, she looked at the display and saw a text message indicator instead.

Barringer: Answer the door.
Calista: What?

She was staring at the phone, waiting for him to respond back when she heard the doorbell ring. She jumped off the bed, walked to the door and looked through the peephole. It was Barringer all right, and he was looking directly at the peephole as if he could feel her doing so.

Calista unlocked the door, opening it slowly to reveal the tall, lean man – her husband. Her breath caught in her throat, in awe of the incredible sight that he was. That he's always been. She first noticed he was wearing jeans again, so right away, she knew he wasn't at the office. He looked so good in jeans, maybe because it was a rare sight for her to see him in casual clothes. And he had on a plain navy blue Ralph Lauren, short-sleeved shirt that showed off his muscular arms. And he smelled good. Oh, how she missed his smell.

She swallowed hard. When she was able to find her voice, she asked, "What are you doing here, Barry?"

"I was in the neighborhood. Why'd you hang up on me?"

She stared up into the depth of his eyes while, at the same time, seeing highlights of their marriage flash before her eyes. She studied his face – the handsome face she hadn't seen in weeks. The last time she saw him, he was angry. This time around, he put off a much calmer vibe, and she could see he'd recently had his hair cut. Mustache trimmed. And he'd shaven. For a second, she thought about running her index finger across his lips but she quickly checked herself.

"You...you were in the neighborhood?"

"Yes. Why'd you hang up?"

She shrugged. "You didn't seem like you wanted to talk, so..."

"May I come in?"

"Um...sure. Okay," she said stepping aside.

Barringer breezed past her to step inside. She thought she would die right there from the heat and intoxicating smell radiating from his body.

"Smells so good," she whispered while closing the door.

"I'm sorry. Did you say something?" Barringer asked, turning to look at her.

"Oh, no. Nothing," she said, nervously playing with her fingers. "Um, so...uh, do you want some chili?"

"Sure."

"Okay. I'll have to warm it up." She walked towards the kitchen, feeling Barringer following her.

He took a seat at the table, watching her work. She'd placed a small pot on the stove and took chili from the refrigerator, heating it up until it came to a boil. She took a ceramic bowl, filling it with chili, but saved room for his toppings. First, she dropped a handful of oyster crackers on top of the chili, stirring them in. Then she sprinkled on cheese and green onions before adding a spoonful of sour cream on top.

She took the bowl and placed it in front of him.

He looked at it.

She looked at him. "Is it okay?"

The corner of his mouth lifted. Looked like he wanted to smile, but didn't, at least not fully. "It's fine. I'm amazed you remembered how I like it."

"You're amazed? We were together for a long time, Barry."

Were together. He didn't like the sound of that. "Yeah..."

She took a Styrofoam cup from the cupboard, filled it with ice and poured him a glass of lemonade.

"Thank you."

"You're welcome," she said sitting in front of him after she poured herself a glass. She watched him take a spoonful to his mouth, followed by a subsequent moaning of pleasure. You know the food was good when it made a man moan.

"Like it?"

"Delicious," he said. "I miss your cooking." He took another heaping spoonful, eating shamelessly.

Calista watched him while he ate, finding pleasure in seeing him do so. While he may not have liked her very well right now, at least he still liked her cooking. "Do you want more?"

He took a drink of lemonade. "I probably shouldn't eat two bowls of chili so late at night, so I'm good. It was delicious by the way."

"Glad you liked it." Calista took a sip of lemonade and held his vision. Then her eyes rolled down to his nose. His lips. Her mouth watered. She hadn't kissed those lips in a long time. She looked into his eyes again and said, "You look like you want to ask me something."

"I do."

"What?"

"You and Garrison…"

Calista's chest tightened. "Yes?"

"How long did you date in college?"

Calista sighed. "It doesn't matter, Barry."

"Maybe not to you, but to me it does. How long?"

"Almost two years."

"And then what?"

"We broke up."

"Who ended it?"

"I did."

"Why?"

"Because I thought he was cheating on me."

"You thought?"

"Yes. At the time, I thought he was, but I learned later he wasn't."

"So it was too late to rekindle anything after that, huh?" Barringer leaned back in his chair and crossed his arms. "Do you still have feelings for him?"

"No. He's my brother-in-law now and I love him as such, but I'm not in love with him."

"Well, you're not in love with me either, otherwise you wouldn't have left me."

"Barry, please don't start with the sarcasm."

"I'm not being sarcastic, Calista. That's the way I feel. Women always talk about men not talking to them and being open with them. Well, I'm being open with you."

"You can be open without being

argumentative."

"I could, but what's the point? I'm not going to downplay the way I feel."

Calista took a sip of lemonade. "Then I can make the same argument," she said calmly. "You left me long before I left you, Barry. I was a lonely, bored housewife for three years."

He hissed his displeasure. "Oh, don't start with that."

"You did. And I tried...tried to be happy, but it was hard to be happy when my husband loved his work more than he loved me."

"Not true."

"It is true. Everything in your life, in Barry's world, took precedence over me. So, by removing myself from the equation, from my viewpoint, you're not missing anything anymore and your life is complete."

"How are we ever going to work this out if you keep rehashing the past, Cali? Or maybe you don't want this to work. Is that it? I'm not your ideal man, so you don't want me anymore. Is that it, Cali? You have someone else in mind? Someone better? And now, you have the freedom to come and go as you please without being accountable to anyone. Why would you want this to work?"

Calista shook her head and closed her eyes. This wasn't going anywhere. And then she heard Candice's voice in her head. *Make an effort.* So, she pulled in a breath, opened her eyes and said, "No, that's not it. I love you. I'm in love with you and that will never change. No one can be as close to me as you. No one will have that special place in my heart but you, Barry. I love you."

Her lips trembled. Eyes glistened with tears. "I have the same freedom in this apartment that I had when I was home. The only difference now is, I *know* you're not coming home because you don't live here, and I'm not waiting with hopeful expectation that you'll be here for dinner, or to watch a movie with me, or hold me at night or have a simple conversation with me for that matter. I know you won't be here. So slowly, but surely, I'm teaching myself to not have hope that you'll change. That you'll realize how lonely I was without you. When I'm here, I'm just here. Not holding out hope. Just here. Alone. I know you're not coming home and it's sad that I'm okay with that, but it doesn't mean I like it. I just don't have a choice," she said, her voice so broken and faint, she doubt if he could make out those last few words she'd spoken.

She took a moment to clear her throat before she said, "Contrary to what you believe, Barry, I don't like being without you. I would prefer being with you. But even when I was home, I wasn't with you. So I'm here, holding my pillow in place of you, crying myself to sleep because my marriage has fallen apart. Because my husband isn't the same man I married, and it hurts me. In hindsight, I see how wrong I was for nagging you about wanting to have a child, but I always wanted children. You knew that. But I think I became desperate in the last couple of years because I needed to have some form of you...some representation of you close to me because I didn't have you. I could love, hug, kiss, hold and take care of a baby...couldn't do that with you because you were never there. You were never there, Barry."

Barringer sat speechless, feeling his heart crumble to pieces listening to her words, seeing tears fall from her eyes.

Calista dabbed her eyes and continued, "And I'm not telling you this because I want you to have sympathy for me, and I'm not crying to make you feel a certain kind of way. I'm crying because I'm hurting." She stood up. "Um...just lock the door on your way out."

Before she could walk by, Barringer reached for her wrist, getting a good grip on her. He stood up and pulled her into his embrace, wrapping his arms tight around her. Finally, it hit home. She needed him. She moved out because he wasn't there. And she was right. He wasn't there. He'd let the company take up all of his time, and all she wanted was him. And now, feeling her crying against his chest, her warm body trembling against his made his heart ache.

He swallowed hard and said, "I'm sorry, Calista. I'm so sorry, baby." He squeezed her tighter. If he held her tight enough, close enough, maybe he could absorb all of her pain.

She sniffled, gently pushing away from him. "I need some tissue," she said, then took off to the bathroom.

From the kitchen, Barringer could hear her blowing her nose. He shook his head. How could he not see what he was doing to her until now? All those nights he'd worked late, stood her up for dinner, all the promises he made but failed to keep – they'd all culminated to her leaving. Now, it was on him to make this right.

He walked in the direction of her bedroom. He saw her there, sitting at the bed's edge, close to a nightstand. He didn't say a word for a moment. He just stared at her – her hair pulled back in a ponytail. She dabbed her eyes while her head hung low.

Not knowing if he could do anything at the moment to console her, he walked her way, stooped down and took one of her hands into his. He felt like he'd died a slow death when his eyes met her sad ones. She was hurt to her heart.

"I don't know what to do to make this right, Calista. It's hard for me to admit that, you know, but I don't know what to do."

Her eyes scanned his features again, his eyes, lips and since he was already holding one of her hands, she took her other hand, grasped his right hand and brought it to the side of her face, closing her eyes as the warmth from his hand soothed her. She missed this. A small smile appeared on her lips. Through the sadness and all, a smile appeared. She opened her eyes again, let go of his hand and gently rested her palms against the sides of his face.

Calista leaned forward, pressing her lips against the tip of his nose, watching his eyes close. She continued leaving soft, moist, gentle kisses all over his face.

"Open your eyes, Barringer."

He opened his eyes and said, "I don't deserve you."

Calista leaned close, leaving his comment in the air as she left soft kisses against his lips.

"Cali—"

"I miss you," she whispered softly against his lips. She proceeded to leave more kisses there until he knew she really did miss him. Until he felt the same things she felt right now. "Do you miss me, Barringer?"

"I miss you so much it hurts, Cali," he said before settling a hand at the nape of her neck, pulling her close to him so their mouths matched up. Locked up. And he kissed her, thoroughly, angling her head from side to side, remembering how good it felt to kiss her with deep, long strokes. Greedily, he suctioned her lips into his mouth and when he felt her desperation, he took her tongue, tangling it with his before taking her lips again. Her whole mouth. And then he felt himself becoming reckless, kissing her all over her face as his breathing thickened.

Settling on her lips again, his hands slithered along her thighs and up her nightshirt while he angled his head in different ways to give her the kissing of a lifetime. He stopped himself, looked at her with desire pooling in his eyes.

"Barry."

"Yes."

"I don't want to hold my pillow tonight."

"Good, because I hadn't planned on leaving."

He stood up, pulled his shirt over his head to reveal a muscle-ripped, chocolate six pack and chiseled chest. He unzipped his jeans, let them fall to the floor, standing before her now wearing nothing but a pair of black boxers.

Reaching for her hand, he invited her to stand in front of him.

Accepting the invitation, she stood up, feeling his hands crawl underneath her nightshirt until he pulled it up over her head, tossing it somewhere in the room.

Standing naked, she wrapped her arms around him. "Oh, Barry. I missed you so much. I miss your smell, your hands, your eyes and your body. I missed you."

"Missed you too, Calista," he said, his fingertips gliding across her back. He pulled the barrette from her hair and immersed his hands into her strands. "Look at me," he told her.

She angled her head up to meet his gaze.

"I love you."

"I love you, too, Barry."

He kissed her again with an intense hunger. He'd been starving for this for a long time now and finally, he had her.

Calista felt like she was having an out-of-body experience, feeling how in depth Barringer was taking her lips, kissing and licking them. His large hands had squeezed and cupped her bottom and she ended up on her back without knowing she was there.

"I know you can feel how much I want you right now," he said, leaving kisses on her neck.

"I know you can."

"I want you too, Barry."

"Do you?"

"Yes," she said desperately. "I do."

"Then want me because you want me and not because you want a baby," he said, and a pained expression touched his features. "I need you to want *me*, Calista."

"You are all I want Barringer Blackstone," she said. "All I'll ever need."

Barringer dipped his head to claim her mouth while feeling her hands explore his body. Squeezing here. Clawing there.

"I need you closer," she said urgently, feeling his teeth graze her neck. "Kiss me, Barry."

She wanted his lips again, so he gave them to her, shifting his body and lowering his boxers at the same time he gobbled up her lips. Then he came down on her, letting the weight of his body restrict her while desire tore through his flesh and made his entire body ache for her.

"You want me closer, baby?" he asked.

"Yes," she said, but it came out more like a desperate whimper.

"How about this close?" he asked nudging her legs apart, easing his body in place.

She held his vision as her body welcomed his and when the overwhelming feeling of him touching the insides of her soul was too much for her senses, she closed her eyes and nibbled on her bottom lip. "Oh, Barry," she whispered closing her eyes and savoring this moment.

His body was large on top of hers, but she welcomed the weight of him. All of him. She needed this – to feel love between them again. And by the way he was making love to her, she knew he needed to feel it, too. "Cali."

She opened her eyes at the sound of her name floating off of his lips. "Yes, Barry," she said, under his spell.

"Make love to me."

Calista looked confused for a moment until she read his glossy eyes. He needed to know she loved him. Regardless. And so she wrapped her legs around him, deepening their connection and opened her mouth wide to kiss him with more aggression than she thought was necessary.

He matched her need, desiring the love he'd been without for so long. He needed this. His body needed this. His mind. His everything.

She gasped, looked at him.

"I'm sorry," he said. A tear fell from his eye that punctured her soul.

"Barry—"

"I'm sorry."

She didn't have to ask why he was sorry. She knew why already.

"I am truly sorry, Calista, but I love you."

"I love you too, Barry."

She squeezed him tighter, locked her legs around him tighter, lifting her head from the pillow to take his lips and kiss him with the same aggression he'd kissed her with until his sadness dissipated. And he reclaimed her mouth again, took control again, while the lower part of him moved slowly. Deliberately.

And then the floodgates opened. She

trembled, closed her eyes and crumbled to pieces. He trembled, let out a rough, loud groan and slumped down over her. They broke apart together as they exchanged unconditional love – the way it used to be in the beginning before life took its toll on them.

The room seemed to be spinning, but they didn't care. They just cared about each other. As the last sensations tore through their bodies, Barringer left kisses all over her clammy face and said, "You don't know how much I missed making love to you."

When she was able to catch a breath, Calista smiled and said, "Oh, I have an idea."

He chuckled softly.

"I missed making love to you, too." She kissed his lips and further down to his chin.

"Let's make this a habit."

Calista laughed through heavy breaths. "Okay."

"Starting right now," Barringer said lowering his body to hers again, kissing her lips while their sweaty bodies crashed together in heated passion.

Chapter 35

Barringer didn't know he could miss the sound of her breathing. As he laid next to her in the morning, he thought about how fortunate he was to have her. He wanted to reach out and touch her face – brush the hair that had fallen into her face back behind her ear, but he chose to watch for now. He wanted to quietly observe and appreciate the woman who would take him as he was – flaws and all. He'd given her a lot to put up with over the years. He wanted to start showing appreciation for her. He would start by making her breakfast in bed.

He eased up, headed to the kitchen to see what she had available in the fridge. He found a carton of eggs. Bacon. It didn't take much to cook eggs, right? How difficult could it be?

He smiled. He'd never cooked breakfast before, not even for himself. Majority of the time, when they hosted family dinners, Calista did all the cooking with him assisting as needed. How did they go through nearly six years of marriage without him serving her breakfast in bed?

He took his time cooking, preparing the meal as best as he could and after buttering some toast, he walked back inside the bedroom with a plate of scrambled eggs, two slices of bacon and a toast. He carried a glass of orange juice in his right hand.

Rounding the door, he saw her lying there, eyes open and her lips transformed into a smile.

"I know you didn't cook breakfast for me, Barry?" she asked.

"I did," he said, setting her plate and cup of juice on the nightstand before leaning down to take a kiss from those lips he'd consumed last night. "Mmm," he said, savoring them all over again. "You know what I realized while cooking this?"

"What's that?" she asked drowsily.

"That I've never cooked for you."

"No, you have not."

"But, that changes, starting now. I may not be a *good* cook—"

"Good or not, I'll eat anything you cook for me, Barry."

Barringer left a kiss at her temple. "Remember that when I bring you something that looks like goulash."

"I'll eat all your goulash," Calista said.

"And you know I'll eat yours, baby," he said taking another kiss from her lips. "Try it." He handed her the plate, watching as Calista took a fork full of eggs to her mouth.

"Mmm...delicious."

He stood up, satisfied and said, "Eat up. You'll need that protein for later."

"Why? What's going on later?"

A grin touched his lips. "If you have to ask, sweetheart, you're not ready. Be right back."

Barringer went to get his plate and was back, eating breakfast with her. "Not bad if I say so myself."

They ate quietly for a moment until Calista said, "Barry."

"Yes?"

"Can we talk about it?"

"What is *it*?"

"You know what *it* is. The baby situation."

Barringer grimaced a little. He didn't want to talk about it, but he knew they needed to. "Yes. We can talk about it."

"I just want to know if you wanted to keep trying treatments."

"I've tried for three years."

She nodded. "I wish you would've told me."

"There were so many times I wanted to. I didn't want to disappoint you, Cali."

"Well, just know I'm okay with it. I love you, and we can be a family, right? Just you and me."

"But I know you want children, Calista."

"I do, but we can always adopt."

"We could, I suppose," he said.

"I wouldn't be opposed to adopting a child. I know I can love a child that isn't mine. I love little Junior. He's not mine. And I'll love all of our nieces and nephews whenever they arrive. And when the time comes and we want to adopt, we'll do that."

Barringer smiled, then finished his meal. "What are your plans for the day, Cali?"

"Um...let's see...it's Sunday. I don't have Junior today, so I don't have plans."

"Good. So we can spend the day moving your things back home, right?"

Calista smiled. "Yes. We can do that."

"Good, because I want to make love to you in *our* bed until we lose consciousness."

Calista felt her breath mingle in her throat. She knew that was a promise he would keep.

Chapter 36

"Barry," Calista panted, barely able to catch her breath. "Don't you...don't you need to go to the office today?"

"Nice try, but I'm not done with you yet, baby," Barringer said kissing her neck up to her ears. "You're too good to let go. You know that?" He covered her lips with his lips, the same way he covered her body with his body. "Mmm, you are so good to me, Cali," he said between kisses. "So good, and I plan on getting the last drop."

She couldn't move. She'd already fragmented beneath him plenty of times. Still, he wanted more. Before she could catch her breath, before the blood could properly flow back to her brain, he wanted her. And he was getting his fill. She was at his mercy.

"Barry, what are you doing to me?"

"Something I should've been doing a long time ago, Calista. Focusing all of my attention on you. Making sure you know how much I love you."

He concentrated on her face as she closed her eyes and nibbled at her lip.

And he plunged, then retreated, over and over again, knowing he was due to send her over the edge.

She grabbed his large shoulders and when sensations zapped through her body, they tore through his at precisely the same moment.

"Barry!"

Her shuddering body locked onto his as her mind went blank.

"Cali," he said in a ragged breath.

"Oh, Barry. I love you."

"Love you, too, baby."

She forced herself to breathe, finding it increasingly difficult to do so while the room was spinning. While the earth broke apart. While Barringer moved his body methodically, in slow motion.

He felt the first waves of desire course through him when he closed his eyes tight and let go, throwing his head back to contain the force ramming through him. This was pure ecstasy.

"Cali!" He grunted, softly calling out her name again next to her ear.

She held on, clenched him. Took him. Made love to him.

The buzzing of the alarm clock filled the room along with their heavy breaths.

"Right on time," Barringer joked, smiling down at her.

Calista laughed beneath him. "Yes, right on time."

THEY PROCEEDED TO take a shower together, making love once more and when they dressed, they headed for the kitchen where she watched Barringer make a protein shake while she peeled a banana. She admired him in his black business suit with a linen white shirt and silver necktie.

"You look handsome, Barry."

"Thank you."

"And happy," she said. "You look happy, too."

"That's because of you. I have my priorities together. And I'm not stressing about the baby situation anymore. What will be, will be."

"Right." She took a sip of orange juice.

The doorbell rang.

"There goes Gary," Barringer said.

Calista smiled, eager to see Junior. She rushed to the front door, opened it and said, "My baby!"

She took the car seat out of Garrison's hand.

"Well isn't this a surprise," Garrison said, taking a step inside rocking a gray suit. "When did this happen?"

Calista couldn't wipe the smile off of her face if she wanted to. "*This* as in me and Barringer?"

"Yes."

"We worked some things out yesterday,"

Calista said.

"I see. You may want to wear a turtleneck for a few days." He smirked, looking at the redness on her neck.

Calista's mouth fell open. "Gary!"

He laughed.

"I'm not paying your crazy daddy any mind, Junior," Calista said, taking Junior from his car seat, kissing him on the jaw. "I missed you, lil' man."

She watched Junior smile.

"Aw, you missed me too, didn't you?" she asked Junior. She returned her attention to Garrison. "I see you're in a suit again."

"Yeah. Now that your husband is sane again, and now I know why, I think we can go back to working together," Garrison said.

"Gary, you better not be in there flirting with my wife," Barringer quipped, stepping out of the kitchen, walking over to where Garrison and Calista were standing.

"Here we go..." Garrison grinned.

Barringer slapped hands with his brother, gave him a half hug then said, "Lookin' good, bro."

"You too. I take it Calista has something to do with that."

Barringer looked at Calista and said, "She has *everything* to do with that." He took a long kiss from her lips.

"I'm glad you guys are back together. Now, Barry and I can handle some business," Garrison said. "You ready, man?"

Barringer brought his hands to a clap. "Let's

do it."

Calista smiled. "Have fun. Me and Junior will be just fine. Say bye-bye, daddy." She held Junior's arm by the wrist and waved his hand at Garrison.

"Can I get a bye-bye daddy?" Barringer asked with a smirk on his face.

Calista puckered her lips and left a kiss on Barringer's lips. "Bye-bye, Daddy."

"Bye, baby. See you this evening."

"Okay."

Chapter 37

"Good morning, Candy," Barringer said, peeping around her office door.

Candice's face lit up, excited to see him back to work after a two-week hiatus. "Barry! You're back!" She hopped up out of her chair and ran to him, hugging him tight right there in the doorway.

"Didn't think you would be *that* happy to see me."

"Why wouldn't I be?"

"Well, you'll be even more shocked to see who I dragged in with me."

Before she could guess, Garrison peeped around the door. "Hey, sis."

"Gary!" she squealed. She looked him up and down. "You're back!" She leaped into his arms and said, "I'm so proud of you!"

"Don't kill me, Candy," Garrison joked.

"I'm sorry. I'm just so excited. Look at you. Did you get a haircut?"

"I did," he said, rubbing his mustache.

"All right, you two," Barringer said. "Meet me in my office in ten."

Candice saluted him. "Yes, sir."

Barringer grinned then headed to his office while Candice walked with Gary to his office.

Garrison walked inside, looked around and said, "Doesn't look like a thing is out of place."

"It's not," Candice said. "Barringer kept it locked. I think he was hoping you'd return."

"And here I am," Garrison said, placing his briefcase on top of his desk.

"Yes. Here you are." Candice watched him open his briefcase, remove some folders and a picture – a picture of himself with Vivienne at the pier.

A small smile touched his lips. He took a long look at the picture and placed it on his desk. He'd taken down all the pictures of Vivienne at home. With Calista's help, he'd packed up her things. But this picture – this picture he needed on his desk. Even when he knew it would hurt to look at it sometimes, he needed it there. "I'll never forget her," he said.

"None of us will," Candice said.

Garrison swallowed hard, pulled in a breath, forcing sadness away.

"So what does Barry have up his sleeve this morning?" Candice asked.

Garrison shrugged. "Your guess is just as good as mine. I rode with him this morning and he wouldn't talk business."

"Wait...you rode with him to the office?"

Garrison nodded. "I did. I dropped Junior

off with Calista and left my car parked there."

Candice grimaced. "Left your car parked where?"

"At Barry's. Are you feeling okay, sis?"

"Yeah. For a minute there, I thought...never mind." She thought somehow in Garrison's explanation that Barringer and Calista were back together. It was only her overeager, wishful thinking. Candice rolled her wrist to check her watch. "How was my adorable, little nephew this morning?"

"He's good...thrilled to see Calista, of course."

"I bet."

"He's going to have to get used to his new surroundings, though. And the place needs to be child-proofed. Maybe you can help Cali with that."

Candice frowned. Now she was really confused. "Okay, wait...the apartment is already child-proofed."

"No, not the apartment, Candy. The house."

"The house?" Candice asked, bright-eyed.

"Yes. The house. You *do* know Barry and Calista are back together, right?"

"They're back together? Calista and Barringer are back together?" she asked, already beaming from ear-to-ear before Garrison could confirm it again for her.

"Yes. Thought you knew that."

"Yes! My prayers have been answered. I'm going to go give that big head man a hug. Be right back."

TINA MARTIN

* * *

"Hey, beautiful."

Calista smiled. "What are you up to, Barry, calling me first thing in the morning?"

"Just wanted to hear your voice, beautiful," Barringer said.

"You used to call me every day. Remember that? When we first got married?"

"I remember. And I'm going to start calling you more. No more taking the woman I love for granted." He leaned back in his chair and took an appreciative look at their wedding photo.

"I'm making dinner for you tonight," Calista told him.

"Good. I miss your cooking."

"You'll be here, right?"

"Baby, I will risk life and limb to be there."

Calista giggled. "Okay, Barry."

"Hey, call Colton and let him know what we're going to do with those bedrooms."

"Will do, and I'll call the cleaning agency to schedule a full house cleaning." I see you've made a mess in the family room."

"That's what happens when a man's life falls apart...when he loses his woman."

"Well, I'm here now."

"And I'm going to make sure you stay. Love you, Calista."

"Love you too, babe."

"See you this evening."

"Okay. Bye."

"Bye." Barringer placed the phone on his desktop, finished ordering the bouquet of roses he was having sent to Calista this morning when Candice barged into his office, smiling.

"I love you, I love you, I love you," she said during a running start before wrapping her arms around his neck.

"What are you so happy about, Candy?"

"You and Calista...you're back together!"

Barringer smiled. "Yes we are, and for good."

"Yes! I knew you could do it."

"Hey, while you're in here, I want to ask you a favor."

"Okay."

"Calista and I have an anniversary coming up. With so much going on, we haven't really been focusing on it, so I want to do something special for her."

"Okay."

"I need your help to pull off a surprise anniversary party at Mom and Dad's."

"That's a wonderful idea. I will get with Mom and plan everything. Don't you worry."

"Thanks. Appreciate it, sis."

After a double-tap on the door, Barringer and Candice looked up to see Garrison peep his head around the door. "Ready?" he asked.

"Candy's already here, so we may as well be," Barringer said. "Come on in."

Garrison stepped in and closed the door. He took a seat next to Candice in the chairs in front of Barringer's desk.

"Gary, not sure if you are aware, but Candice and I had a meeting with representatives from The Champion Corporation – the company Blakeney went to. Desmond Champion came here to meet with us along with Kurt Hempstead, the guy Candice couldn't stop gushing over."

"Stop your lying, Barry," Candice said, withholding a smile.

"He better be lying," Garrison said.

"Ugh," Candice grunted, red in the face. "Thought we were getting down to business."

"We are," Barringer said. "So, The Champion Corporation wants to make BFSG a division of their company."

"And Barry turned them down," Candice chimed in to say.

"I did, but I think we need to take our time and think this through. I'll admit to being a little hasty before, but if the situation with me and Calista has taught me anything, it's that I can't make life-changing decisions without consulting all parties involved. So we're going to talk about this thoroughly...need to find out everything we can on the Champion brothers."

"Okay," Garrison said. "I went to college with a Champion."

"Was it Dante, Dimitrius or Desmond?" Candice inquired.

"No. The guy I know is Harding Champion. Real smart, techy type."

"Hmm...wonder if they're related." Candice said.

"Not sure, but I can find out," Garrison said.

"Candice, since you and Kurt seemed to hit it off, you work that angle."

"I'll call him and use my influence to get the scoop."

Garrison frowned at her.

"What? I'm a grown woman, Gary. Gosh. You and Bryson kill me with that overprotective stuff."

"Wait until Bryson finds out you got a crush on this Kurt fellow," Garrison said.

"It's not a crush," Candice said, unable to stop smiling. "And now that I have my assignment, I'll be going to my office. *Adios* boys."

"See ya later, Candice." Barringer said.

After Candice exited, Garrison asked, "So you think this move with The Champion Corporation might be a good thing?"

"I think it's worth looking into. I don't want to hand out pink slips to these hardworking people here."

"Me either."

"Then we'll take our time and make a decision. It's not we need to resolve this overnight."

Garrison nodded. "Well, in the meantime, I'll work up some numbers. Blakeney has been gone for four months, and I know we've gotten new business since then. Let me get to work...need to see how much of a hit we're taking."

"Okay, Gary. I'll have Eleanor put a meeting on the calendar for this afternoon so we can discuss your findings."

"Make it for three o'clock," Garrison suggested.

"Got it."

Garrison stood up to head to the door.

"Oh, and Gary."

"Yep," Garrison said, turning around.

"It's good to have you back, bro," Barringer said.

"Good to be back." He proceeded to his office, eager to get to work.

And Barry laid back in his chair and glanced at Calista's picture. He ran his index finger across her face. He meant what he told her earlier. Taking her for granted was a thing of the past. From now on, she would know she was first place in his life.

Chapter 38

Garrison secured Junior in his car seat then headed to the door. In his other hand, he carried a plate of food that Calista had set aside for him. She would always remember to do so whenever she cooked. Her brother-in-law wasn't going to survive on fast food.

Barringer threw his hand up before he drove away. Stepping back inside the house, he inhaled a deep breath, pulling in the aroma of a home-cooked meal – fried chicken, green beans, homemade biscuits and mashed potatoes. Boy was he glad his woman was back home.

"Have a seat, Barry. I got everything under control in here," Calista said from the kitchen.

He could see her moving around in the kitchen. While she worked, he sat down at the dinner table, paying attention to the four, lit pillar candles in the center of the table along with the red roses he'd sent to her. Soft music played in the background.

"Sweetie, you don't need me to do anything."

"No, hun," Calista said, stepping into the dining room with a small basket of biscuits. She placed the basket on the table before walking over to stand in front of him. "Barry," she said, lifting his chin with her index finger.

"Yes, sweetheart."

"Thanks for the roses. They're beautiful."

"You're welcome."

"Do me a favor," she said.

"What's that, baby?"

"You're home now. Loosen your tie and kick off your shoes. Relax."

Barringer did what she asked, even came out of his suit jacket.

She brought the chicken and the rest of the meal to the dining room, then took a seat close to him.

Barringer grabbed a chicken breast and took a huge bite.

"Mmm," he moaned. "This is the best."

"Miss my cooking, huh?"

"That, and everything else about you."

Calista smiled. She proceeded with preparing plates. "Candice called me, elated we're back together."

"She's been over the moon since I told her."

"I told Kalina. She was *over the moon*, too. Seems everyone thinks we're good together."

"We *are* good together. I'm never letting you go again, Calista. I mean that."

"Good, because I don't want to be *let go*."

* * *

Barringer walked out of the bathroom with a thick, white towel wrapped around the lower half of his body. He saw Calista sitting at the vanity, wearing a silk camisole, brushing her hair in long strokes. Through the mirror, she could see him walking in her direction. Sometimes it was hard for her to believe the tall, sexy, muscular man was hers.

Her pulse quickened when he took the brush from her hand and asked, "May I?"

A small smile touched her lips. "Yes. You may."

He proceeded to brush her hair in the same long, slow strokes as she was brushing it. He didn't know why he was making sure her strands were even, making sure her hair was neat when he had plans to mess it all up again.

"Calista."

"Yes?"

"What did you miss the most about us when we were apart?"

"I missed you. Missed being in your arms."

He placed the brush on the vanity and reached for her hand.

She took his hand and stood up, after which, he pulled her into his embrace.

"You missed being in these arms?" he asked, pulling her close to his chest, his chin resting on top of her head.

"Yes. These arms, Barry." She released a satisfying sigh, because she was home, and it felt good to be home. So good.

"You know what I missed the most about you?"

Calista smiled when she said, "Besides my cooking?"

He smirked. "Yes. Besides that."

"No. What?"

"Talking to you. Making love to you." He looked at her, placed his hands on both sides of her face before leaning down to take a small kiss from her lips.

Her eyes closed when she felt his lips around her mouth, lingering there. Even when they'd made it to the bed, his warm body hovering over hers, he kissed her lips longer than he had ever kissed them, making up for lost time. He had a lot of making up to do.

While he focused on her neck, his hands did their own exploration, fingers skimming across her soft skin, up and down plump curves.

"I never knew how perfect you were for me."

Calista giggled. "Oh, stop it, Barry."

"I'm serious," he said, holding her gaze to emphasize how serious he was. "I love everything about you. From this beautiful head of hair," he said, while running his fingers through it, "To those pretty little toes. As a matter of fact, let me go say hi to them."

Calista laughed. "Barry, what are you doing?"

His towel fell off as he kissed his way down towards her feet. He massaged her toes, kissed them softly before kissing his way back up her legs, feeling them quiver. He lingered at her breasts, using her moans and whimpers as motivation to continue his kisses. And then he couldn't take it anymore. He needed to make love to this woman. His woman.

With his iron-clad body looming over hers, he connected their bodies, nearly losing consciousness at the feel of her. And to think he almost lost this...

That feeling would always be at the forefront of his mind every time he looked at her, every time he kissed her and every single time he felt heat between them like this.

Calista closed her eyes, enjoying the feeling of him claiming her soul, loving how his body felt on top of hers. He was all the man she needed – all the man she would ever need. She brought her hands up to his face, pulling him down towards her to meet her lips while wrapping her legs around him at the same time.

Barringer kissed her harder as he moved his body slowly enough to drive her insane. Enough to drive them both to the edge of senselessness. Her muscles spasmed and his groans became thick immediately before their bodies shattered together. She held on to him when he wouldn't let up. No. Not yet. He wasn't done just yet. He kissed her more, stayed the course until she felt sensations stir inside of her all over again, until they both used up all the oxygen in the bedroom.

"Are you okay?" he asked through ragged breaths.

"No." She laughed.

Barringer wiped sweat from her forehead.

"You look okay."

Calista laughed, still catching her breath. "Do I?"

"You do." Barringer pulled her close to his chest.

"Barry."

"Yes, sweetheart?"

"Do you realize we have an anniversary coming up?"

He smiled, thinking about the surprise party he had planned for her. "Yes. Number six."

"Six years." She reminisced on all of those years, good and bad, thinking that she wouldn't have wanted to share her life with anyone else. Only Barringer. "We should go somewhere?"

"Go somewhere?"

"Yes. When was the last time we went somewhere? I think a weekend getaway is well deserved."

"And where would we go?" Barringer asked after he left a kiss at the nape of her neck.

"We don't have to go far. We could rent a cabin in Nags Head."

"Really?" he asked playfully, kissing her back.

"Yes. Really."

"And what would we do in this cabin?"

"You'll just have to wait and see."

Chapter 39

Barringer stepped into his parent's home looking at the decorations, the candles, flowers, the elegant place setting on the table and the red, pink and white balloons clinging to the ceiling. Excitement hung in the air as the family hurried to put the finishing touches on the decorations and food before Calista arrived with Junior.

After he'd looked over everything and gave his approval, Barringer took position at the window, keeping lookout for Calista's arrival.

"Nervous?" Bryson asked Barringer.

"A little," Barringer admitted. "She may decline my request this time."

Bryson chuckled. "That's not likely. If she came back after everything y'all been through, I doubt if she'll be leaving again. Breathe easy, brother." Bryson patted his brother on the shoulder before he walked off.

Barringer sucked in a breath. Why was he nervous all of a sudden? It wasn't like him to be nervous about anything. And the past week with Calista was one of the best weeks they'd shared in a long time. But Calista thought she was coming to a family dinner when really, she was going to be hit with a surprise anniversary party.

"Distracting her with Junior was a good idea, huh?" Garrison asked as he tossed a ham and cheese pinwheel inside of his mouth.

"It was," Barringer said. "Good thinking, man."

"I knew she wouldn't decline a chance to spend time with him."

Barringer grinned. "You're right about that."

"Be right back. I have to get some more of those pinwheels," Garrison said.

"They *are* good, aren't they?" Candy said.

"Yeah. Where did you get them?" he asked. "Costco?"

"No. Kalina made those."

"Then I hope she knows she'll be making another batch real soon," Garrison said, heading for the kitchen.

Candy laughed, then wrapped her arms around Barringer. "Looks like everything is all set, care bear. You ready to sweep your girl off of her feet? Again?"

"I'm ready." Barringer peeped through the blinds again and saw Calista taking Junior from the back seat. "Everybody, get ready. She's here."

"Are we supposed to hide?" June asked.

"No, June," Kalina said. "It's not that kind of party. Calista knows we're all here, but she doesn't know it's a surprise party. So let's stand right here in front of the door, so when she opens it, she sees everybody. Then we'll all yell, *happy anniversary*. Once her mouth falls open in sheer surprise, we'll let Barringer take over."

"Got it," June said.

"All right, everybody. Let's go to the foyer," Candice said. She walked to the kitchen to take her mother by the hand. "Mom, Cali's here."

"Oh, well, let's go," Elowyn said.

And now, they were all standing anxiously waiting for Calista to open the door. Everson stood next to June, but he was so busy on his cell phone, he probably didn't know what was going on. June nudged him and he still didn't bother to look up at her.

Bryson stood behind Kalina with his arms around her. She placed her hands on top of where his hands met. "It's nice we can all get together and appreciate each other again," he said, leaving a kiss at her temple.

"It is," Kalina responded. "You know how important family is to me."

"I do. That's why I can't wait to start on our own."

Kalina smiled and squeezed Bryson's hand.

Candice wrapped her arms around Garrison and said, "I love you, Gary."

Garrison smirked. He knew what she was doing. Knew this was probably difficult for him since losing Vivienne and all, but still, he made an effort to support Barringer and Calista. "Love you too, Candy."

Theodore stood next to Elowyn. They were

all smiles.

Barringer rubbed his hands together when he heard Calista talking to Junior.

The moment had finally arrived. When the doorknob turned and Calista entered with Junior, everyone yelled, "Happy anniversary!"

Calista's eyes shot open along with her mouth. "Wh-what are you guys doing?" she asked, completely shocked, looking around at all the decorations and the family standing there.

"I'll take this," Garrison said, taking the car seat from her hand and removing a smiling Junior from it. He couldn't hold him for five seconds before Elowyn was taking him away.

"Barringer, what is all of this?" Calista asked.

"Well, since it is our anniversary, I thought I'd throw a surprise party for you, with the help of the family, of course."

Calista placed her right hand on her chest. "Everything is so beautiful." Her eyes swelled with tears. "Kalina, Candy, and June...where was my warning that this was coming?"

The women laughed. "Not this time, sis," June said.

"Besides, Barry wanted it to be a surprise," Candice said, looking at Barringer.

Calista looked at him, too.

Everyone looked at him.

Barringer took Calista by the hands. "I did want it to be a surprise because you deserve it. And, I just want to say thank you for putting up with me all these years. I know I've been a pain to deal with at times and I'm sorry, I'm truly sorry my actions drove you away, but I'll never allow that to happen again. I love you, Calista."

Tears rolled down her face when she said, "I love you too, Barry." She wrapped her arms around him briefly before he dropped to one knee.

The family erupted in cheers and applause.

"Then you would do it all over again?" Barringer asked, staring up at Calista.

"I would."

He removed a ring from his pocket, a three-stone diamond ring that sparkled beneath the lights and said, "Calista Blackstone, will you stay married to me?"

Calista smiled and said, "Yes, Barringer Blackstone. I will stay married to you."

Barringer placed the ring on her finger until it met the ring she already had there. He stood up, wrapped his arms around her before lowering his mouth to leave a kiss on her lips.

"This is truly wonderful," Elowyn said.

"Amazing," Candice added, awestruck as she observed real love. She couldn't wait to fall in love to experience all of it – the ups and downs – good and bad times.

"That's so sweet," June said, pinching tears from her eyes.

Kalina stole Calista away from Barringer, admiring her new ring.

Theodore walked over to Barringer and said, "Well done, son."

"Thanks, Dad."

"I've learned, over the years, that when a

woman is worth it, you have to do what you have to do to make it work and keep her happy. A tall order, but hey, it can be done."

Barringer nodded. "You and Mom are living proof of that."

"Yep," Theodore said, exhaling deeply while glancing over at Elowyn.

Barringer looked over at Calista as she laughed with the women while they took turns admiring her ring. And, as if feeling his stares, Calista looked up and caught his gaze, holding it for a long time.

He smiled at her.

He knew they had a long way to go to repair their marriage. He was ready to travel that road because, like his father said, when a woman is worth it, you make it work. Calista was definitely worth it, and he would spend the rest of his life making her happy.

* * * * * *

Missed Kalina and Bryson's story? Get a copy of EVENINGS WITH BRYSON today!

EVENINGS WITH BRYSON
(A Blackstone Family Novel)

What happens when a woman who doesn't believe in love meets a man who's given up on love?

Kalina Cooper has been hiding her loneliness by drowning herself in work at her home office and continuing on until the late evenings at her Aunt Edith's café. Her 'happily ever after' doesn't involve a husband. Having seen her father walk out on her mother when she was a teenager, she doesn't believe in love.

After a bad divorce from a cheating woman, Bryson Blackstone vows to never marry again. But he never expected to cross paths with a woman like Kalina Cooper. She's different. She's special. From what he has learned about her, he knows she doesn't believe in love, but he doesn't know why. Now he plans to weasel his way into her life to find out, because Kalina Cooper is just the woman he'd consider if he was crazy enough to fall in love again.

On sale now wherever books are sold.

Amazon Top 100 Bestselling
Author
TINA MARTIN

invites you to discover The Champion Brothers
Series!

Book #1
HIS PARADISE WIFE
Widower, Dante Champion, has his eyes and heart set on Emily Mitchell, but she's not interested. She's falling for a man she met online. When she discovers her mystery, online man is none other than Dante Champion, will a weekend at Pleasure Island change her mind about him?

Book #2
WHEN A CHAMPION WANTS YOU
Melanie Summers is not ready for a relationship, but a possible new job at The Champion Corporation puts her center stage in front of Dimitrius Champion. They've exchanged glances before, but hardly anything more. But will a straightforward proposition from Dimitrius interfere with her chances of landing a dream job and real love?

Book #3
THE BEST THING HE NEVER KNEW HE NEEDED
Bad boy, motorcycle-riding, alpha male, Desmond Champion, is the youngest of the Champion brothers. He's had his mind on Sherita Wilkins more times than he'd ever admit. A business deal brings them together, but it may be Desmond's selfish ways that drives them apart.

On sale now wherever books are sold.

www.tinamartin.net

Enjoy Tina Martin books?

Check out other titles by the author below.

Mine By Default Mini-Series:
Been In Love With You, Book 1
When Hearts Cry, Book 2
You Belong To Me, Book 3
When I Call You Mine, Book 4
Who Do You Love?, Book 5

The Accidental Series:
Accidental Deception, Book 1
Accidental Heartbreak, Book 2
Accidental Lovers, Book 3
What Donovan Wants, Book 4

Dying To Love Her Series:
Dying To Love Her
Dying To Love Her 2
Dying To Love Her 3

The Alexander Series:
The Millionaire's Arranged Marriage, Book 1
Watch Me Take Your Girl, Book 2
Her Premarital Ex, Book 3
The Object of His Obsession, Book 4
Dilvan's Redemption, Book 5
His Charity Challenge, Book 6

Non-Series Titles:
Secrets On Lake Drive
Can't Just Be His Friend

All Falls Down
Just Like New to the Next Man
Vacation Interrupted
The Crush

For more information about the author and upcoming releases, visit her website at www.tinamartin.net.

55623137R00188

Made in the USA
Columbia, SC
16 April 2019